About the author

Craig Micklewright grew up in the West Midlands and now lives in Wales. He has enjoyed writing as a hobby for much of his life and over the years has studied and developed his flair for creating worlds, characters and scenarios. He works as an I.T. Technician and is also a keen movie enthusiast. He has now published several novels that have become the realisation of a lifelong dream. Favourite genres include crime thriller & horror.

Also by

Craig Micklewright

Dying Games Saga
Showdown In Los Angeles
The Dying Game
Gemini
The Fallen

Available now at Amazon

(also available on Kindle)

FOREVER MIDNIGHT

By

Craig Micklewright

Copyright © 2023 Craig Micklewright

All rights reserved. This book or any portion thereof may not be reproduced or used in any manner whatsoever without the express written permission of the publisher except for the use of brief quotations in a book review.

This book is a work of fiction. Characters, places, events, and names are the product of this author's imagination. Any resemblance to other events, other locations, or other persons, living or dead, is coincidental.

ISBN: 9798377452676

I

She reclined on a soft leather couch, an afternoon sun creeping in through half drawn blinds, creating a pinstripe shadow over her swollen, out-sized belly. The fabric of her dress stretched into prominence as her long legs reached across the couch; feet free of the restraint of shoes, and her left hand brushed out a crease in the fabric.

Patricia Willis looked to an older man seated in a high back leather chair just a couple of feet from the couch, dressed well in a tweed jacket, white shirt, brown trousers and good shoes. He was about forty-eight, maybe fifty, she thought, his slightly receding hairline giving him away where a tanned skin and probably cosmetically refined wrinkles had masked him.

She had turned 29 earlier in the year, but felt older. The man's learned eyes examining her as if trying to figure her out; something she had become accustomed to doing herself. Patricia had made some questionable decisions in her relatively young life; nevertheless, one she didn't regret was all the more evident as she lay there, presented to this man for inspection. He wasn't interested in her appearance though, he was more interested in her mind, and how she was feeling, as any good therapist should be.

"So Patricia, how did you feel when you first discovered you were pregnant?" He asked.

Patricia sighed, letting her head fall back, her cropped hair pushed back with a blue hair slide. Despite how she was feeling, her face was blossoming like it often did in most women in such a condition, and her make-up was minimal, creating a fresh-faced, somewhat juvenile appearance.

"Oh, I don't know. I was pregnant once before…" She replied.

"Oh yes? Tell me about that." The therapist responded.

"It didn't stick around long enough for me to feel much of anything. It was more than a year back… I miscarried, or at least, that's how I like to think of it."

"You lost the baby? I'm sorry to hear that. May I ask what happened?"

Patricia closed her eyes. She didn't like to recall, and her silence told the therapist the memory was painful.

"Maybe we'll come back to that another time. So, you were telling me about how you felt, about this pregnancy…"

Patricia's thin lips curved into a smile as the soft sunlight bathed her face.

"It wasn't a mistake. I didn't plan it. But when I knew it was real, I told myself, God had given me a second chance, that it was meant to be."

The therapist looked pleased.

"A close friend and I spoke about it for a while after we found out, and it was going to be perfect."

"And then what happened? You told me earlier that you are not with the father."

Patricia opened her eyes, but preferred not to make eye contact.

"You know, I always hated how cold and clinical that term sounded 'the father', like he was just some *thing* that put this child inside me, like somebody just filling a purpose, and not a man, not somebody I cared for."

"I'm sorry; I didn't mean it to sound like that. Please accept my apology, Patricia."

Patricia smiled again, before sitting up. She turned and dropped her feet to the oak flooring, then slowly raised her head to focus her striking sapphire-blue eyes on his face.

"It's alright. I don't mind talking about it. That was an important time for me. It was a stepping stone. I wouldn't be who I am today, if this hadn't happened." She announced, her tone slightly more upbeat.

The therapist nodded, clearing his throat.

"I'd say we're making good progress here, Patricia. We have a few more minutes. Why don't you tell me about Miami? You moved there earlier in the year, is that right?" He said.

Patricia bowed her head and looked at her feet as they brushed against one another.

"Yes. That was when it all began." She replied quietly.

Miami, Florida
Wednesday 23 July

A man in his early forties, sporting a perfectly contoured beard and bleached blonde hair, inserted a key in a lock of an apartment door. Patricia, her hair shoulder-length, wearing sunglasses and a simple two-piece suit, waited patiently behind him.

"You know, this is the first time I've been to Miami." She said optimistically.

The man smiled, "I find that very hard to believe."

"Well, when I say first time, I mean, that I can remember – apparently we came on vacation here when I was about three."

The man opened the apartment door inwards and stepped inside, dragging a large suitcase in with him.

"Welcome to my crib." He said, and held an arm out, beckoning her to enter.

Patricia looked into a hallway, nicely decorated, but nothing that special. She glanced at him for a moment, then walked in.

She soon entered a living room, and looked around at the leather furniture and paintings of country-side scenery hung up on the walls, along with a large plasma TV above a marble fireplace. She was pleasantly surprised.

"Hey – I like it! How long you been here?" She asked.

"About six months, give or take. Bit of an upgrade from my last digs. But this ain't the half of it… follow me." The man continued, and walked back out into the hall, as Patricia followed him, until they entered a kitchen, which was bigger than the living room, and equally as impressive.

"I know it might not be that big of a deal to a rich kid like you, but I haven't really had a place like this in years. It came furnished, with full air conditioning."

Patricia glanced around, and smiled. *Darren's done pretty well for himself*, she mused.

"Can I see *my* room now, Darren? You are aware we're not sharing a bed." She teased, smirking.

Darren chuckled back to her, "Don't worry, it's this way." He replied.

A door opened into a small room with a single bed. A window to one side led out onto a balcony, and long, red drapes moved in the breeze.

"What do you think?" Darren asked, standing with Patricia as she inspected the room with intrigue.

Patricia then turned to him, and sighed, "Darren. Can I say something?" She asked.

Darren examined her face with his eyes, "Yes, of course."

"You know this is just temporary, right?"

"What do you mean?"

"Staying here. If this works out, then I'll want a place of my own. You do understand that, don't you?"

Darren smiled, "Hey. That isn't a problem. I'm just trying to make you feel welcome."

"This hasn't been easy for me, you know."

Darren glanced away from her to look back out into the hall, "Listen. I know how much of a risk this might seem to you. But you need to know, I have no hidden agenda here." – he looked at her again, "You are a good Detective. Yeah, you have had your problems. God, I can sympathise with that much, but like anyone in our world, we gotta go back to what we do best – and this is you, Patricia… it's who you are."

Patricia felt touched by his words, and began to really feel a connection with this man who had been absent from her life for more than four years. She looked around the room again, then approached the bed. She dropped a purse onto it and looked back at Darren again.

"Would I be able to take a shower?" She asked, "After that flight, I think I could do with feeling human again."

"Sure. Make yourself at home. I'm gonna step out for a half hour, somebody I gotta talk to – you gonna be alright until I get back?"

Patricia nodded, slipping her shoes off next to the bed, as Darren left, leaving the door ajar.

"Seems everything has worked out just fine, then." She quietly said to herself, starting to unfasten the front of her suit jacket.

Minutes later, Patricia stepped under the spray of a shower, and ran her hands back through her hair, eyes closed as she kept her mouth open to playfully taste the water. It had been such a long journey. She had never been a fan of traveling. Being away from home had made her nervous, but it wasn't as if she hadn't experienced any of it before, it was just that, well, this was such a big step for her. Was she really ready?

Darren had said he would not be long. She was tired but also frustrated, her natural urges going unsated for far too long. Patricia had not given herself an orgasm in over a week – and that need within her loins was becoming unbearable. Yet in the relative seclusion of the bathroom, she knew that, even if Darren came back unexpected, he wouldn't dare walk in on her, not with the sound of the shower to warn him. She dropped a hand to her crotch and cupped it. Damn, she was on fire down there. It would be quick, but memorable, and she so needed release. Her head rest against the Perspex of the shower door as she let her mind wonder, which was easy in her state of bewildered over-tiredness.

Gently, she toyed with the loose folds of her labia, before finally finding her clit, already pulsing with a hint of the pleasure that awaited her.

She then felt something that caused her to frown. A thick wetness coated her fingertips. Without warning, stomach cramps doubled her, and she fell against the inside of the cubical. Raising her hand for inspection, her eyes bulged when she discovered blood. *This didn't make sense*, she thought, suddenly feeling light-headed. Her period was only a couple of weeks ago. In addition, there was more than usual. She then held up both hands to witness thick blood as it ran freely from large gashes to her wrists. Overwhelmed at such a horrific sight, she became unsteady, grabbing at a rail fixed to the wall to stop herself from falling. Her head was spinning. Quickly she slid the door open and made for the outside, yet caught her foot on the lip of the shower floor, gasping as she fell, landing on her front, half in and half out of the cubical.

The sudden violence of the moment was enough to slip her into unconsciousness.

II

Darren Maitland entered an old brown-stone office building a few blocks from his apartment. It was a respected law firm, and an attractive blonde woman immediately greeted him. She was wearing a grey two-piece suit and matching high heels.

"So, where we heading?" She asked with enthusiasm.

"Had a decent morning?" He replied.

"Yeah, kind of." She answered, her mood changing slightly, "The er… Valmont case is gonna be banging in my head for the next few weeks … but I'd rather not talk about it right now. Let's go eat."

Her name was Sarah-Anne Hartshorne, a 32-year-old second-year law student at the highly respected *Boomer, Burns & Brunt* firm, which was pretty much the law capital of Miami next to the local Police department, and had handled several high-profile cases.

"Well, I was thinking of that place over on *Melody Park*, the Spanish eatery that's recently opened."

Sarah, her shoes compensating for the fact she was a little shorter than Darren, looked into his eyes, and smiled.

"That sounds great, babe. I was thinking, maybe I will stay over tonight, if you'd like me to, that is." She replied with a glint to her eyes and wrapped her arms around him.

Darren stared at her, taking a moment to think, "Well, there's a bit of a problem with that. Since I've been back, I kinda got company, a tenant you might call it."

Sarah frowned, "Well, that's alright, surely he can make himself scarce for one evening…"

"I suppose, but it's like this. She's an old friend, and it being her first night in a strange town an' all…"

Sarah took a step back, screwing her face up, "Wait a minute, it's a girl? You've got a girl living with you all of a sudden?"

"Hey. She's not a girl, she's a woman, she's er… 28, a friend … but … there's nothing going on!" Darren retorted nervously.

Sarah did not know how she was supposed to feel. Why did he want another woman there when he had her, friend or no friend? Moreover, why did he need a tenant? He was pretty well-off financially speaking.

"I need some air." She replied quietly, then walked briskly to the glass doors, and exited.

Darren sighed, watching as she left, then cursed to himself.

One hour later

Darren and Sarah walked up the corridor and stopped at the apartment door. Sarah looked a little bemused but had agreed to come along with Darren, at least to clear the air by meeting this 'Patricia'.

"So, how long you and this woman been buddies?"

"Up until recently, I hadn't seen her in years. But, she's a good detective. H&T could use her talent."

"I'll bet." Sarah mumbled under her breath.

Soon the door brushed the carpet, and Darren entered the hallway, and could hear water running.

"Patricia? You in?" He called, and walked up the hall, then stopped at the bathroom door, opposite the entrance to the kitchen.

He listened, but the sound of water was too loud.

"How long has she been in there? Check out the steam…" Sarah remarked, and came to stand beside Darren, who looked down to see steam filtering out around his feet, and the carpet had become damp.

"She said she was gonna take a shower – but that was a while ago now." He said.

He turned to the door and rapped his knuckles against it.

"Patricia? You OK in there?" He called.

No reply came.

"Hey, is she alright?" Sarah asked with sudden concern.

"I'm beginning to wonder." Darren replied, and tried the handle.

"Wait. Your friend isn't gonna be too impressed if you go barging in there. She could be in the middle of washing her… bits. Let me go." Sarah then said, and pushed Darren aside.

She tried the handle and the door clicked open. As it swung inwards a cloud of steam flooded the hallway.

"Jesus. It's like a Turkish bath!" She exclaimed, waving a hand in-front of her, then stepped forward, before stumbling.

"Hey. You alright? Sarah?" Darren called, keeping out of view behind the door.

After a long pause, Sarah replied, "I think you better call an ambulance."

Darren looked stunned, then peered inside, and could just make out Sarah, on her knees, then on the floor, lying naked and not moving was Patricia.

"Oh God, no…" He gasped.

*

Patricia raised herself from a squatting position next to a four-poster bed. It was dark in the room, and she had a funny, metallic taste in her mouth. As she went to move, she almost over balanced and looked down to find herself wearing tall high-heeled shoes, the type she had always had trouble with. Carefully she approached the far end of the room, searched for a way out with one hand, then hesitated as a fly passed by her face. She wrinkled her nose at a horrible smell – like rotting flesh. She gripped a doorknob, turned it slightly and the door, clicking on release, opened and flooded the room with light. It was then she glanced at the bed, and cried out at seeing a fresh, human carcass – its exposed ribcage seeming to let off steam, and more flies buzzed around it hungrily.

Patricia opened her eyes to see a kind face peering down at her. At first, she found it difficult to adjust to reality.

"Ah, she's awake." He said, then went out of view.

She could hear a machine bleeping continuously, in time to her own heartbeat. A brief pause came and went, then she heard the familiar sound of Darren's voice.

"Patricia? Can you hear me, honey?"

Patricia sighed, grimacing with discomfort and she tried to change position, but a hand came to her shoulder.

"Don't try and move, Miss, you're going to be a little weak – you lost a decent amount of blood and we had to administer a transfusion."

She guessed the hand and voice belonged to a doctor.

"We found you in the bathroom, I was so worried." Darren added.

"I don't understand." She groaned.

"Don't worry, the doc reckons you are going to be fine." Darren said reassuringly.

Sarah stood at the bedside with Darren, staring at Patricia with concern, as Darren spoke to the Doctor. *Helluva way to meet*, she thought.

"Can we take her home?" Darren asked.

The doctor looked at Darren, then walked to the door, taking Darren with him as Sarah watched, then glanced to Patricia again.

"Excuse me for asking this, sir, but has your wife a history of this sort of thing? You see she is not on our records, so we haven't been able to run any checks."

Darren frowned, "Excuse me? She's not my wife, doc. But no, as far as I understand, this is completely out of character."

The doctor returned his attention to Patricia, who was looking increasingly worried.

"Maybe it would be a good idea to keep her overnight, for observation. To be honest, she's very lucky to be alive. However, I'd say she should be back home and safe by tomorrow."

Darren nodded, looking to Sarah then Patricia. He returned to the bedside.

"Well, maybe I should let you rest now. We'll come back in the morning." He said.

Patricia smiled at Darren, then focused on Sarah.

"You going to introduce me to your friend?" She asked.

"Oh… yes, of course, this, erm…"

Sarah interrupted, "I'm Sarah – Blake's fiancée."

Patricia frowned, "Blake?" She retorted, as Darren stared at her sternly.

She looked back at him, before recalling something. She saw herself turning over a card held in her hand, to read: 'Blake Thomas, P. I.'

She cleared her throat, "Oh, yes, so… you guys are, er, together then? You old dog, Blake – why didn't you tell me?"

Sarah looked at Darren accusingly, "Yeah, you old dog, why didn't you tell her?"

Darren just returned his best innocent smile.

III

As night fell Patricia lay awake and restless in her hospital bed. That clinical smell such places always exuded never sitting comfortable in her nose. Confusion also lingered as to the actual reason she was there at all, unable to get her head around why or how she could suddenly have cut herself. Never in her life had she experienced suicidal thoughts, at least not seriously; the question of her own sanity starting to invade her mind like a parasite.

Rolling onto her back, she pushed the covers down, then reached for the sensors taped to her. They peeled off easily, much to her relief, as it had felt so violating knowing that little bleeping machines were keeping an eye on her. *Anyway, the doctor did say I was going to be ok, right?*

The door opened to her room, and she peered out into a long, shadowy corridor. Patricia felt a tad vulnerable in just a flimsy hospital gown, and the tiles were ice cold to her feet. The outer corridor was silent and eerily lifeless, although it gave her an opportunity to go and explore a little. If anyone saw her, she could always say she was just hungry or something.

Venturing onwards, she felt like a prisoner making their daring escape, although she had no real intention of doing so. Yet the prospect of sleeping felt alien to her in such surroundings, so a walk was as justified as anything else.

Soon she reached an office, where a window gave whoever was inside a clear view down two other corridors. Pausing at the door, Patricia went to grab the handle, until she heard a noise. Listening carefully, she frowned at what she thought was a gentle moaning. She stepped forward to the window, and slowly brought her face to the framework, until she could peek inside. She then had to clamp a hand over her mouth to stop herself from gasping.

Inside was an orderly going by his uniform and, kneeling on the floor, between his spread legs was a young nurse. She was pleasuring him with her mouth, and by the way he had his head tilted back, she was doing a more than decent job. Patricia couldn't believe her eyes. She watched the woman sucking and licking the man's erection with expertise, and going by the way the shaft glistened, the bulbous head throbbed and the noises coming from the orderly - ejaculation was imminent.

Patricia forced herself away. If she stayed when he reached the point of no return, he might see her, and then what? She was never any good at lame excuses for doing something she shouldn't. Quickly she moved to the other corridor, and hurried on tiptoes down it, then reached a door. Suddenly she looked back in alarm just as a light in the office came on, and in reaction Patricia opened the door, disappearing inside.

Patricia stood within a darkened room with her face up against the door until her nose was almost touching the wood. Her heart was pounding in her chest and an incredible guilt flooded through her. She began to regret leaving the relative safety of her room. Then, she heard a voice.

"Hello? Who are you?"

Patricia turned on her heels, and her back pressed against the door as she spotted a young woman sitting up in bed. She appeared naked due to her top half being totally on show, and just a thin sheet concealed her lower half. She had long, flowing black hair, a pretty round face with prominent cheek bones, and perfect, perky breasts. For a moment, Patricia forgot how to speak.

"Oh, you've seen them too..." The woman remarked.

Patricia looked at the woman who, she guessed, was probably early twenties. Her dark eyes and pale skin were distinctive and appealing in all the ways Patricia tried to deny.

"Seen who?" Patricia finally replied.

"That guy and Nurse Elizabeth. They're lovers, ya know." The woman added, strangely unconcerned with displaying herself like she was.

Patricia was tempted to point it out, but was also afraid she might listen and cover herself up.

"You've seen them together?" - Patricia's eyes jumped quickly from the woman's breasts to her face, hoping she hadn't been spotted staring.

"They think I don't know, that I just lie here ignorant, but I tell you now, those two, they fuck almost every night."

Patricia was shocked by the woman's ease at saying such an expletive.

"What's your name?" Patricia then asked.

"*Lisa*. What is yours?"

"Erm, it's Patricia."

"They'll be done soon. Elizabeth works the night shift, but *Gary*, that orderly is only on until twelve. Why don't you come and sit down, keep me company? I don't sleep too well."

Patricia looked around the room, which was pretty indefinable, with just moonlight coming in from a barred window to light Lisa up. Patricia smiled, then approached the chair beside the bed, sitting down.

"So, why you in here?" Patricia asked.

"I did something silly." Lisa replied with a childlike pout to her bottom lip.

"What do you mean?"

"I slashed my wrists."

A brief silence lingered in the room.

"Hey, don't worry, that's not something I'm going to be doing again any time soon, and anyway … he won't let me."

Patricia was confused, "Wait. Who's he? Who won't let you? The doctor? Your father?"

"The demon." Lisa then answered abruptly.

Patricia's eyes widened, "Come again?"

The woman then raised her hands to show the bandages. They looked very similar to those adorning Patricia's own wrists.

"The doctor's they said I had lost so much blood; I really should be dead. But I couldn't carry on anymore, I couldn't be that creature's vessel. So I thought if I died, it would free me – but no, that wasn't going to happen. I'll never be free, the demon has much bigger plans in mind."

Patricia did not know where to put herself, the night turning out to be quite eventful.

"You can't be serious. There's no such thing as demons. Surely you know that, don't you?"

She stared at Lisa who lowered her arms, turning her head to look away. Her long dark hair moved in a breeze Patricia wasn't previously aware of.

"Well, don't you? Why did you cut your wrists?" Patricia added, in need of an explanation to her own situation as much as that of the woman's.

Lisa then mumbled something under her breath.

"Excuse me?" Patricia said, frowning.

Lisa sighed, before suddenly turning to look at her with glowing yellow eyes.

"Because of the murders!!!" She cried.

Patricia's eyes sprung open to see the machine beside her bed bleeping rapidly. Her heart was beating like a train rattling down the track. She was back in her room. For a moment she just lay there, on her side, staring. As if realising it had been a dream, she quietly whispered to herself.

"My God – what is happening to me?"

Gradually the heart monitor returned to its regular speed.

At Darren's apartment, Sarah wearing a simple robe showing she had stuck with her offer to stay over, entered a study, a small room with bookshelves, where she found her fiancé seated at a desk in front of a PC. She placed a coffee she had made on the desk as he handled a cordless mouse, the flat screen monitor lighting his face as he perused his e-mail inbox.

"Blake? Can we talk?" She asked, the steam from the coffee dancing in the light from a table lamp.

"Just a minute. I'm checking my mail."

Sarah sighed.

"You understand why I was a bit surprised by your lady friend being here."

Darren clicked on an e-mail, where the subject read: 'Possible new case'. He did not open it, but turned in his office chair to look at his fiancée.

"Of course I understand. But I couldn't tell you about her, in case it didn't work out."

"What do you mean?"

"When I took that trip over to LA, I didn't know whether or not Patricia would be interested. She's had a few things go on in her life between now and the last time she was involved. I half expected her to have moved on."

"Are you sure she's entirely, you know… 'stable' ? She just tried to kill herself, didn't she?" Sarah added.

"Hey!" Darren snapped, "We don't know nothing. Talk like that is not helping anyone – least of all Patricia. Let's wait and see what she has to say before we jump to conclusions. Patricia is a good person. What happened was nothing like her – there's going to be a reasonable excuse for what she did. Patricia will explain everything when she comes home."

Sarah smiled, realising she was reacting without really knowing Patricia at all. She came closer, and wrapped her arms around Darren, until his head nuzzled her chest, then as she lay a kiss on his head, she felt him undo the belt of her gown, and it fell open, exposing her body presented in her best silk lingerie. A small butterfly was tattooed on her abdomen. Sarah grinned as she let Darren kiss her breast, her head falling back as she groaned with pleasure.

"Let's go to bed." She breathed.

IV

Thursday 24 July

The following morning, Patricia sat in the passenger seat of Darren's Honda HR-V, peering out of the window as buildings blurred the horizon. He kept glancing at her as he drove, a quiet tune playing on the in-car CD.

"You going to be alright?" Darren asked, concerned.

Patricia looked washed out, the complete opposite to the fresh and lively woman from the previous day. She held her cell phone in one hand and was checking her messages. She noticed she had received one from her younger sister 'Cameron'.

"I guess. I just need to get back, change my clothes, figure out some stuff." She mumbled.

Darren then turned off the main road, heading into the suburbs.

"There's been an interview arranged at the agency. You gonna feel up to attending? It's tomorrow morning at ten." He said.

Patricia's thumb hesitated from pressing on the text message, her relationship with Cameron never easy.

"An interview? But I thought…" She replied, and sat up straight, pocketing her cell phone.

"Well if it had been up to me, the job would be yours, but David, the agency's owner, he's a bit reluctant to hire someone he hasn't at least spoken to first."

Patricia nodded, "I guess that's reasonable. I'll be there, you can tell him."

Darren looked to Patricia for a moment then re-focused on the road as she noticed.

"What?"

"You understand – I gotta ask." He said.

"Alright, before you start accusing me of being a suicidal freak show – all I know is that I just started bleeding – I don't know why it happened – It just… did. I can't explain it."

A melody then began playing, and Darren answered the incoming call via the car's dashboard.

"Blake Thomas." He answered – the name still sounded so alien to Patricia.

"Blake. It's David. Did you get my e-mail?" came a man's voice.

"Oh, yes. Shit, I haven't looked at it yet – kinda got sidetracked. What's this case you're talking about?"

"Bit of a strange one I'm afraid – the local PD haven't exactly been helpful, but we have a couple, whose daughter was involved. They turned to us after the Police put up a wall of silence."

"Go on…"

"Just get over here. We have to begin work on it immediately."

"Well, I'm kinda with someone right now." Darren added.

Patricia looked over, picking up on an Australian accent.

"Sarah can hang about whilst we…"

"Not Sarah."

"Who then?"

"That old friend I told you about."

"*Patricia Willis*? She's here, now? Crikey." came the man's surprised reply.

Patricia suddenly felt like a celebrity.

"Yes." Darren confirmed.

"Then bring her along! I guess it's as good a time as any for me to meet her. If she's as sharp as you say, we might need her."

Darren sighed. He was hoping to work Patricia gently into the equation. David obviously had other ideas.

"We'll be right there." He concluded, then ended the call with a tap of a button on the car's steering wheel.

He glanced to Patricia, then made a sharp turn, and pulled the car around to drive back in the opposite direction.

"Darren! You can't be serious. I'm a mess. I need to get changed, freshen up at least." She remarked, startled.

"You heard him, he wants us both at the agency right away."

Patricia pulled the passenger sun-guard down, checking her appearance in the mirror.

"I'm not ready for this." She added.

"Well, too bad. Sounds like he has a big case for us. If we don't get over there right now, he could pass it over to one of the others."

"Others?" Patricia asked.

"Maybe I should tell you, that the agency is nothing like you were used to back in New York."

"Oh?"

"But never mind that right now. Just focus. There's a comb in the glove compartment, and a bag of mints. That should do for now – and keep those bandages out of sight – we don't need David anywhere near that shit. Oh, and another thing…"

"What?"

"Get out of the habit of calling me *Darren*. You are the only person here who knows that name. You better start using *Blake Thomas*, or this thing is over before it's even begun."

Patricia sat feeling incredibly nervous. She had not felt this way in a long while. Was she sure she had done the right thing, coming over to Miami and leaving her family? Yet, as she thought to herself, she knew life wasn't going to just grab her and slap her across the face to make her do something important – she had to take any opportunity that arose, and if that included risking everything – then so be it.

*

A little while later, an elevator door opened in an office building, and Darren walked in with Patricia, who was taken back by the grand, plush interior and the countless people dressed well and rushing about.

"My God." She remarked.

"Bit of a change from *Narrow Eye Investigations*, huh? This is a big concern here. Lots of nasty cases in Miami, you see." Darren mused.

"You don't say." Patricia replied, continually pushing the cuffs of her blouse down to hide the bandages, until Darren noticed and nudged her.

"Just relax." He whispered.

From one office, a tall brown-haired man in his mid-forties appeared, and held out his hand. Patricia instantly found him attractive, his skin perfect, probably treated with various lotions, his dark eyes hinting at something she couldn't quite put her finger on, whilst his open collar shirt offered a glimpse of something she rather wished she could.

"David!" Darren announced.

"This must be Patricia!" David said, and took Patricia's hand firmly, "David Henderson. Nice to finally meet you."

She smiled awkwardly at him, and they made eye contact for longer than was strictly necessary.

"Hi." was all she could say, immediately feeling foolish, *Yep, definitely an Aussie.*

"Come! I have all the details in my office." David said, and pulled Patricia forward.

She looked at Darren briefly, until she was ushered away.

As Darren followed them into the office, the door closing behind them, a woman seated on a sofa in the middle of the outer office, turned to look. It was the same person from Patricia's dream, all black hair and exotic beauty. She smiled mischievously to herself, then got up and walked away.

Inside, David walked around to the other side of a large desk, and took a seat. Darren sat down in the only other seat available, whilst Patricia was left standing at his side. At first she glanced to him, but thought it wise not to remark.

"So, this had better be good, David. I wanted to spend the day with Sarah." Darren said.

David looked to Patricia briefly, then pushed a file across the desk to Darren.

"Check out these photographs I managed to get off a contact of mine at the Miami P.D."

Darren noticed how serious David looked, and turned the file around before him, then opened it to the first page. He was shocked by what he saw.

"Oh my…" Patricia remarked.

The photograph that they were presented with, was awash with the colour red. It was a shot of a woman, in some kind of black gown, perhaps silk, the cause of death unclear.

"What am I looking at here?" Darren asked with revulsion.

"We know her as some supposed psychic, although she is thought to be a fake." David explained, "Rumour suggests she was a member of some kind of cult. Going by the state of the hotel room, it's strongly believed to be far from a *Christian* thing. Quite the opposite in fact."

"We talking devil worship? I thought that kinda shit was reserved for *New Orleans* and bad b-movies."

David smirked. Darren then turned the page, and gasped when he saw a wall, where a pentagram; a five-pointed star was painted in blood, above a bed. Chains and handcuffs were displayed across the mattress, and copious amounts of blood soaked the surrounding floor.

"Holy fuckin' Christ." He exclaimed.

Patricia had to look away.

"Twelve women, all found dead. No stab wounds or nothing. It's just as if they hemorrhaged through their mouths and noses. I tell you now, this one has affected me. I've never seen anything like it." David added.

Darren cleared his throat, closing the folder, "Wish I could say the same." He mumbled, and Patricia suddenly looked at him – he had gone a frightening white.

"Er, *Blake*… are you OK?" She asked.

David stared at Darren also, and then took the file back.

"Care to elaborate?" He asked.

"About six years back. I was involved in a case; murders all linked to some kind of satanic ritual … the pentagram being a factor in each." He explained, with some difficulty.

Patricia looked concerned.

"I'm sorry. I never knew that." David replied, "I'll understand if you don't want anything to do with this – but listen to me..."

Darren looked at him sternly, "What?"

"If you have seen this kinda thing before, then this case might greatly benefit from your input. We still have the young girl to interview."

Darren sighed, running a hand over his face and back through his bleached hair.

"I don't know. What's the story with the girl?"

"She was kidnapped, about a week before any of this happened. Everyone believed she was gonna wind up wrapped in a bin liner and dumped in a lake."

Patricia looked at David.

"But she was found at the hotel. She's eight years of age, Blake. This kinda shit is gonna wreck her for life. If we leave it to fester, she'll be a closed book."

"Let me talk to her." Patricia interrupted.

David looked to her, as did Darren.

"Excuse me?" David replied.

"Let me interview her. I think it's for the best, being a woman."

"I'm sorry, Miss Willis… but have you got any experience with kids?"

"Have you?" She replied, instantly regretting her slightly attacking tone.

David didn't reply, staring at her like an interfering stranger.

"Give this to me. I know I can do it!" She continued, realising she'd fare better not backing down.

Truth be told, Patricia did not really have much experience with children, but she felt bad for what the girl must have experienced - must have seen. She wanted to help, in anyway she felt she could.

David sighed, relaxing back in his chair, "I don't know. I understand you've done and seen a lot, Miss Willis, but this is a particularly delicate case."

So was the Ellie Marie and Raymond Campbell case, so was the Jane Andrews killings. I have the experience, David… you can ask Blake – he knows."

David looked to Darren.

He smiled, "She's good, David – I told you that much. She's a better Detective than I ever was."

Patricia was a little taken back by how he worded such a compliment. David just stared at her, before finally responding.

"Ok. Nevertheless, this isn't a trial thing. You mess this up, Miss Willis, and that's it, the case is as dead as those twelve women."

Patricia nodded then smiled back, "Trust me." She replied confidently.

V

David walked down a corridor with a young couple and their eight-year-old daughter; a shy, nervous looking blonde girl dressed in a blue tracksuit. The woman held her by one hand as they proceeded.

"We have hired a child psychologist to sit in with us – I hope you don't mind, Mrs Winters, Mr Winters…" David announced, as he came to a door, which stood ajar.

The couple, in their late twenties, shook their heads, looking equally as nervous as the girl.

"Now don't worry about a thing, Jessica – these people are here to help." Mrs Winters said, peering down at her daughter, who didn't respond, staring at the door for some reason.

"If you will…" David said, and pushed the door open, stepping aside to allow the couple to enter.

Inside was a small room used for certain interviews, and was less intimidating than David's office. There was no desk, just a group of chairs, and seated with one leg crossed over the other, was Patricia. She was wearing a finely tailored suit with a split at the skirt, exposing a little more thigh than David approved of; and had tied her hair back and put on a pair of spectacles to give the perfect professional image. Seated to her left, was a man with a moustache and receding hairline, holding a clipboard, his straight face and beady eyes in stark contrast to Patricia's elegance.

"Please, take a seat." David offered, indicating the chairs with his hand, and the couple walked over to them, moving them back before sitting down. Jessica climbed onto her mother's knee.

"Hi. My name is Patricia. Nice to meet you." Patricia said.

Mr Winters glanced to the man with contempt.

"We love our daughter." He then said.

Patricia glanced at David.

"Close the door will you, David?" She said, and he did as she asked, resting with his back against it.

"I'm sure you do, Mr Winters. It's Jessica, right?" Patricia replied, turning her attention to the girl.

The girl glanced at her for a second before looking away.

"She's been through hell and back. What good is this going to do?" Mrs Winters said, her young face free of make-up and her eyes looking tired and blood shot.

Patricia stared at her sternly.

"If we are to have any hope of understanding what happened yesterday morning, we need to talk. You know we are trying to discover who was responsible for your daughter's disappearance, yes?"

David cleared his throat, grabbing Patricia's attention.

"Tone it down." He whispered.

Patricia was offended. She took a breath, thinking to herself, and picked up a file from the floor, opening it on her lap.

"This may be difficult for you, Jessica, but I have some photographs here, and I'd like you to tell me what it is they show."

Mr Winters looked troubled, "I don't know – she just wants to forget … what photographs?"

David stared at Patricia – he had not been told about this.

"It's alright. We have decided not to show her anything too traumatic. Just a couple of pictures we're puzzled about."

David cleared his throat again, but this time Patricia did not respond, taking a photograph from the file, and leaning forward.

"Jessica, honey? I'm sorry. I understand how scared you feel. But if we are to help apprehend the people responsible, you need to help us." Patricia said with a gentle tone to her voice.

Mrs. Winters stared at her, then looked to Jessica, who raised her head to look at Patricia. Jessica's large, elfin eyes returned a blankness that echoed her recent trauma.

"They're all dead." She replied in a sweet voice.

Patricia just smiled at her.

"Can I show you a picture?" She asked.

The girl nodded. Patricia then turned the photograph over to show a blood-stained wall where unusual writing in a strange language was scrawled. The girl stared at it with fear.

"It's their way of talking – it's what they say…" She whispered.

Patricia leaned closer as the couple looked increasingly concerned. The child psychologist made notes on his clipboard.

"What do you mean 'it's what they say'?" Patricia urged.

The girl looked up at her, "It's how they bring the dead back…"

Patricia was shocked. David approached and held out his hand.

"Give me the photographs." He ordered.

Patricia was focused on the girl's face, "Hold on – we're getting somewhere here."

"No. I didn't agree to this."

"Just let her see the next picture." Patricia added, swapping the photographs over with her hands, and held the next one up.

It showed the burnt outline of a figure lying on a blood-soaked carpet.

"What is this?" She asked.

Jessica stared at it and went wide-eyed.

"It's her!!" She gasped, then turned away to nuzzle her mother's breast.

Jessica's Mother held her tightly.

"I think that's enough!" She snapped, and Patricia sat back.

"I'm sorry." She replied and handed David the photographs.

Suddenly, Jessica began to convulse, and shook violently in her mother's arms. Mrs Winters looked alarmed, and Mr Winters got up from his seat.

"What's happening? Jessica, baby! It's Ok – you're safe here!" He announced, panic-stricken.

Patricia got up also, and the psychologist came to her side.

"She's having some sort of seizure!" He exclaimed.

He rushed to the child's aid and took her from Mrs Winters' arms to lie her on the floor.

As they stood around her, with the psychologist crouched at her side, the jolting and shaking grew more violent, white liquid foaming at her mouth.

"Oh my God!" Patricia gasped.

David didn't know where to put himself.

"Should I call an ambulance?" He asked.

The psychologist looked back, nodding.

"Let me!" Patricia then said and rushed to the door.

She sprinted down the corridor, entering the main room, and rushed into David's office, startling Darren who was pouring himself a drink at a bar in the corner.

"Patricia?" He exclaimed.

She grabbed the receiver off the desk and dialed 911.

"Who you calling? Is everything alright?" Darren asked.

Patricia just turned away.

Back in the room, the psychologist was trying to restrain an uncontrollable Jessica as she twisted and turned her body on the floor, screaming and yelling.

"This is no seizure!" Mr Winters said in alarm, then as he knelt down to try and calm his daughter — blood suddenly splattered his face, and the psychologist stumbled back, crashing into the chairs.

A distressed David looked at the suddenly still girl to see blood soaking her face where her nostrils and mouth had hemorrhaged. He quickly looked away, unable to handle what had just happened.

Soon in David's office, Patricia concluded her phone call, then looked to the door as it opened. The psychologist peered in.

"Miss Willis, the girl, she's …"

Patricia noticed a look of hollowed-out remorse in his eyes.

"She's dead."

Darren looked at Patricia whose eyes widened in disbelief.

"No!" She retorted, and rushed out of the office, but Darren went after her, grabbing her around the waste just as she saw David stumble out of the other room.

"Hey, hold up there!" Darren gasped, and Patricia fought in his arms, before turning away, burying her face in Darren's chest as she burst into tears.

Darren just stroked her hair as he made eye contact with a traumatised-looking David.

*

A short while later, Darren left his office at the agency and went to walk up the corridor until he met up with David.

"Hey." David said.

Darren just looked at him.

"Have you any thoughts on what happened back there?" David asked.

Darren shook his head, "She was just trying to prove to you she had it, that she had what we're looking for. She's good, David."

David nodded, "I guess so, but I think there's stuff going on here we don't really understand."

"What do you mean?"

"An eight-year-old girl doesn't just bleed out for no reason, and neither do a dozen women in a motel room. It's fucked up."

"You can say that again."

"Earlier, you mentioned an old case, involving pentagrams – this might be a good time to elaborate." David added.

Darren stared at him, "I was just rambling. It was nothing."

"No, Blake… you were reminded of it, because of this case. You should tell me about it."

Darren turned away, "Understand something, David. If I do not want to talk about something, it is no disrespect to you, but if I'm secretive … *then I have my reasons*. We'll solve this case regardless."

David frowned, and then watched Darren walk away.

In one of the other offices, Patricia sat slumped over a desk, her hair draping her like a shroud. She was then alerted to her cell phone vibrating against her breast, and slowly raised her head to retrieve the phone from her jacket. Brushing her hair away with her other hand, she revealed a flushed face, her eyes giving away the fact she'd been crying. Looking at the screen, another message had been received from Cameron. With a sigh she opened it.

'Hey Sis,

Did you see my last text? Just checking in on you. How's Miami? Hope your new job is going ok. Anyway, ring me some time. Miss you xx'

Patricia smiled, and typed back, 'Sorry I've been swamped. Miami is beautiful. Chat soon x'

Short and sweet. She pressed 'send' then placed the phone on the desk. There was no point in burdening her little sis with her problems, yet was relieved that her taking off so suddenly hadn't caused another rift between the two of them. She went to finish her coffee, then grimaced at its cool texture. A knock then came to the door, and she looked over.

"It's open." She shouted.

David entered and approached the table, taking a seat opposite.

"Patricia. Can we talk?"

Patricia looked away, placing the coffee aside. *Oh here we go*, she thought, *we're not looking to hire anyone just yet… yada yada.*

"What is it?" She eventually replied.

David reached a hand out and touched hers, "Don't beat yourself up over this. It wasn't your fault." He said.

She focused on his hand as it covered hers, and the effect was soothing. She noticed a glimpse of bandage peeking out from the sleeve of her jacket. She retrieved her hand instantly, praying he hadn't noticed.

"I'm so sorry … I-I really wanted to make a better first impression. This has been a disaster." She said, quick to conceal both hands under the table.

"You surprised me, that's all. But when you were talking to that girl, even though it scared me, I couldn't help but be impressed."

Patricia looked at him, relieved, "Seriously?" She responded, expecting a thorough telling off along with her marching orders.

Yet there was a kindness to his eyes.

"You need to know, I've done my research. Blake has filled in the blanks, so I already knew what I was getting when he said you were coming onboard with us. Your reputation precedes you, Patricia … but I am willing to accept the good with the bad."

Patricia sat back, trying to appear calm.

"So, what now?" She asked after a long pause.

"You've seen enough for today – go home, and we'll start afresh tomorrow." David replied, much to Patricia's surprise.

"Hmm … yeah, I don't think I'll be any further use to you today." She concluded.

VI

Patricia arrived back at the apartment without Darren, who had chosen to stay and help David with the impending questions and answers session they expected from the local PD. She inserted the key Darren had given her in the door, but to her surprise found it unlocked, and with caution, proceeded into the living room. A TV was on showing that someone had been there recently, and a plate with some cold toast on it was sat on a coffee table in the middle of the room. She sighed, forgetting for a moment that Sarah might be home. She went to call out, but for some reason stopped herself.

Walking back into the hallway, Patricia crept towards the bathroom, which stood a little way open, and went to peer inside. The interior was lifeless, although a light was on and a shower had been run recently going by the beads of water still running down the inside of the cubical door. Patricia sighed, feeling stupid – what was she doing? Sarah and herself hadn't even spoke to each other and already she was hoping to catch sight of the pretty blonde in the all together?

Patricia, feeling foolish just headed for her room, then stopped in her tracks when she heard a muffled moaning. Puzzled, she glanced to Darren's bedroom door, and slowly approached. Pausing at the crack in the hinges, she peered in with the knowledge that she wouldn't be seen, and then her eyes widened at what was presented. Lying on a double bed, naked and with a towel under herself, was Sarah. She was running one hand over her petite body, squeezing her breast, whilst her other hand rapidly rubbed her shiny-wet pussy, evidently close to orgasm. The way Sarah was contorting her face, complexion flushed added to the visual Patricia was treated to. Then suddenly, Sarah bucked, a high-pitched shriek escaping her mouth as she raised her bottom from the bed, and her fingers pressed into her puffy opening.

Patricia had to step away, her thong having grown wet in the process, and the temptation to touch herself had almost been too much. She then gasped as a floorboard creaked under foot, and before she could find out if Sarah had heard, she hurried away to her own room, closing the door behind her.

Sarah lay on her back with her eyes wide, breathing starting to calm. She *had* heard, and going by the sound of a door closing, it had not been Blake, the dirty git would have burst straight in if it had been, just like the last time. Slowly, she moved her hand from the stickiness of her crotch, rolled over, and dropped her feet to the floor, wrapping the towel around herself. She looked to the door and noticed the light coming in through the crack at the hinges. She exhaled, her head still a little spaced out as she got up, securing the towel with a tuck just above her breasts before walking out to the hallway.

In the other room, Patricia stood in almost total darkness. She had taken a moment to compose herself, feeling guilty at watching something she herself considered private and personal, and tried to ignore the tingling in her own loins as a result. Slowly, she walked to the balcony doors, and pulled the drapes open to brighten the room.

Someone cleared their throat. Patricia turned around to see the beautiful black-haired woman sitting upright on her bed, wearing a leather jacket, a short mini skirt, an old dirty-looking t-shirt and black, laddered hold ups with high heels.

"You… again." Patricia gasped.

"It's her, isn't it?" The woman replied, "I believed it was you – but no, it's her."

"You're not real." Patricia added and looked away.

"I had convinced myself that he had found someone new – someone worthy. But if it's not you, then that's OK. I can handle that other woman – she could barely handle herself. Call that an orgasm? She hardly knew what she was doing."

"Get out." Patricia said quietly.

A breeze fluttered the drapes, making them brush Patricia slightly. After a few seconds, she found the courage to look again – but the woman had vanished.

Soon Patricia walked into the kitchen to see a fully dressed Sarah making some tea. Sarah did not look at her, and Patricia took a cup out from a cupboard above the sink unit.

"Want one?" Sarah asked.

"Yeah, ok then, thank you." Patricia replied.

She placed the cup on a draining board and watched Sarah wait for the kettle to boil. It was the most uncomfortable feeling, both knowing but neither of them daring to mention it.

"So, anything interesting happen at the agency?" - Sarah finally said, ice breaking like a Polar bear was standing on it.

"Oh…" Patricia replied, and could not believe how what had happened could have fallen from her mind so easily.

"What is it?" Sarah asked in concern.

Patricia looked at her, then turned away, walking over to a dining table and pulled a chair out. She sat down, and Sarah approached.

"Hey, you can tell me – did something go wrong?"

"Wrong? That's an understatement."

Sarah sat down next to her and leant one arm on the dining table surface. Patricia raised her head and looked into her pretty, previously unnoticed green eyes. Sarah was quite eye-catching and even more attractive close up. She began to think what they had shared, be it unintentionally, had suddenly brought them together.

"A little girl died today." She admitted with difficulty.

Sarah looked shocked, "My God that's awful. I'm so sorry… how did it happen? Who was she?"

"She had suffered so much, and had been kidnapped by some twisted cult. We still don't quite understand how it happened. Darr – I, er … Blake will be speaking to Police along with David, so I was told to go home."

Sarah seemed to examine Patricia's face with her eyes, and it made Patricia tingle slightly. If it was not for Darren, she thought, she could quite easily fall for such a girl.

"Sarah… I just…" She stammered, then suddenly, Sarah leaned forward and lay an open-mouthed kiss on Patricia's lips.

Patricia responded, reaching a hand up and curling it around the back of Sarah's neck as they kissed like lovers, their sudden insatiable lust completely out of control. Patricia pulled away; she looked at Sarah with absolute shock. Had what just happened really happened? She suddenly become intensely attracted to the woman, even wanting to kiss her – yet the actual reality seemed to fragment within its own surreal emotions. Sarah was looking confused.

"What are you looking at? Are you alright, Patricia?" Sarah asked.

Patricia stared at her, then forced herself to look away.

"I… I think I'm going to lie down for a bit." She replied, then got up and walked away, leaving Sarah alone, and with a smear of saliva across her mouth.

Back at the agency, two black cars with blacked out windows were parked half on the sidewalk at the front of the building. Police tape had closed off the entrance, and Darren stood next to a leaning palm tree that formed part of the wide-open road's extravagant look.

David walked out onto the street and ventured over to him, as two suited men wearing sunglasses, talked in the background.

"They say it could be a couple of days before we can open up shop again. Shit, I shoulda seen this comin'." He complained, as he held a cigarette, lighting it and taking a drag.

Darren's hair fluttered in the slight summer breeze generated by the traffic that drove by, some slowing down to take a look and wonder what had happened.

"The kid was our only lead. Maybe we should pull a few strings and take a trip over to that hotel room." He remarked.

David passed him the cigarette, and Darren took a drag himself.

"Whatever went down there I think it's gonna stay with those that died. No witness left alive for us to question… the whole thing seems hopeless."

"Nothing is ever as open and shut as it at first looks, David – remember? Let's see what we can take from the crime scene, and go from there."

David looked at him, but felt the situation was already hopeless. However, he did appreciate Darren's optimism.

"So, when did you and this Patricia meet?" He asked.

Darren dabbed some ash off the end of the cigarette, then passed it him back, "It's been over four years. We worked together for a short period. She used to run a Detective Agency in New York."

Darren wasn't comfortable talking about the past. He felt it was a time in his life he would rather forget. Pity Patricia had brought it all flooding back by just being here. Yet it was a regret he was willing to accept if she proved to be as good as he thought she was.

"Oh? How old is she? 25?"

"She was 28 in February – Valentines Day to be exact. She was just five month's shy of her 24th birthday when she arrived in the big apple."

David looked impressed, "23 and suddenly a detective. How'd she spring that? You say she was rich? Did she have any experience?"

"Most of what I know about her I have learnt researching her in the past year or so. We only knew each other briefly, but I'd like to think we made a connection. How else would you explain her being here?"

"I guess so. So, had she studied crime in college?"

"She has a bachelor's in law. Her parents wanted her to follow in their footsteps and become an attorney. She didn't want that, so decided to leave LA and I guess … find her calling."

David watched a pink Cadillac drive by with some cheer leaders in the back. It was an eye-catching sight, but nothing all that unusual for Miami. He smiled, already forming a picture in his head of Patricia's life, to go with everything he knew about her professionally. He was liking what he saw.

"I said she could start afresh tomorrow. I think if we can go to that hotel, it would be as good a place as any – and it's probably been cleaned up enough not to freak her out after today."

"Agreed. You gonna call your contact in the P.D.?" Darren asked.

"Yeah, I sure am." David replied with renewed confidence.

VII

Darren returned to the apartment a few hours later as it began to get dark out. Checking his watch, he entered through the door into the hallway, then removed his jacket just as Sarah exited the bedroom. She was wearing a business suit having not long returned from the office.

"Oh, your back then?" She said, a file in one hand and a mug of coffee in the other.

"You been swatting up on that case?" Darren asked.

"I went over to the firm to see if I could have some reading to take home. You don't mind me doing a little here tonight? I always get restless at my place – on my own."

"No, that's fine. Hey, come here will you?"

Sarah smiled and approached, until they met up by the living room door.

"I'm glad to see you are alright with this now."

"I know. I've had time to speak to Patricia. She seems erm... nice." Sarah answered.

"I knew you two would get along. You know, she has studied law and was once going to be in the same line of business as you are."

"Oh really?"

Patricia then came out from the living room, pushing gently past them. She stared at Darren with curiosity.

"Don't mind me. I just need the bathroom. Did everything go OK at the agency, Blake?" She asked as she walked towards the bathroom door.

"Yeah – we'll talk about it later ok, Patricia?" He retorted.

Patricia smiled back at him, but appreciated he would want to be with Sarah for a little while first.

"No hurry." She replied, and disappeared inside as Darren looked into Sarah's eyes, before following her into the living room.

*

Sarah rolled onto her back as she lay beside Darren in bed. Darren was sound asleep as she glanced at the digital clock on a table next to the bed. It was 11:57pm. The prospect of sleeping seemed to have escaped her; her thoughts and emotions feeling all mixed up. Perhaps it was something to do with what had happened between herself and Patricia. On the other hand, maybe she should not have studied right up until she went to bed.

Entering the bathroom a few seconds later, she lifted her satin slip and sat down to urinate into the toilet. As an aching that had been in her bladder began to ease, she pictured Patricia asleep in the room Darren had given her, her presence at first unwelcome but now it proved a frustration, her sexual identity suddenly in question. Taking some tissue from a roll on the wall, she wiped herself, before getting up and flushing.

Soon she walked into the living room, and a jacket was there she had discarded earlier. It was her favourite, a corduroy overcoat with nice deep pockets and a belt. She had had it for a few years. Picking it up, she looked to a clock on a wall near her, then gasped as the hand turned midnight. Suddenly, she pulled the jacket on and looked around herself. For some reason she felt claustrophobic, and needed to leave, not tell Darren, not get her clothes, just get out.

She left the apartment, and closed the door, wearing the long jacket over her flimsy slip, her bare feet vulnerable on the cold tiled floor of the outer corridor. She didn't care though, the feeling of being trapped becoming almost unbearable, and she only understood that she had to get away – quickly.

Sarah ventured out onto the street a few minutes later and hurried away from the apartment building. A few people passed her by, giving her strange looks, but she chose to ignore them. None of them mattered. The night was warm though, so even her lack of clothing meant little.

Eventually she entered a side street out of sight from the still rather bustling roads and populated sidewalks. In her haste she had become breathless, pausing by a fence to catch her breath. After a moment, she became aware of the sound of high heels. Looking up the dirt-track walkthrough, she spotted an ebony-skinned woman pacing around beneath the glow of a neon sign. There was an entrance to a wine bar, somewhere Sarah and Darren had gone on occasion, but she hadn't thought much of the place. She was also aware prostitutes frequented the area. Going by this woman's minimal attire of hot pants and a leather jacket, she certainly fit the stereotype, likely waiting for some loser to wonder by. Sarah thought she might intervene.

Walking up to the woman, who had dyed red hair and was of similar build to herself, Sarah offered a smile as she caught her attention. At first the woman said nothing, smoking a cigarette, then stepped aside as if to allow Sarah to enter.

"I'm sorry…" Sarah then said, not moving.

"Excuse me?" the woman replied, then looked at Sarah properly.

Sarah's jacket was unfastened and her satin slip visible beneath.

"I can offer you money." Sarah then said.

The woman looked confused, "What was that? You alright, honey?"

Sarah took a purse out of her jacket and opened it to reveal various bills lining the interior.

"Two Hundred bucks – what do you say?" Sarah added.

The woman looked her up and down, "Sorry lady, but I don't follow – you trying to pick me up? And what's with this – you be almost butt naked!"

Sarah looked down at herself, rubbing one bare foot against the other, then stared at the woman again, "Does it really matter?" She asked.

The woman frowned, then looked at the purse again, "Add another fifty and you've got a deal, honey. Shit, been a while since I shared my bed with a girl." She said.

Sarah smiled, closing her purse and pocketing it, "Done – let's get out of here."

"I have a room above this joint – let's go upstairs. There is a private entrance around the back."

Sarah just looked at her, and then followed as the woman began to walk away, high heels echoing in the night air.

Soon Sarah was led into a small room above the wine bar, and had removed her jacket. The woman watched her with curiosity as Sarah walked over to a bed with a dull lamp above it that lit up the mattress, and revelled in the way the slip barely covered her pert round bottom.

"I gotta say," the woman announced, playing with a thick band of gold on her middle index finger, "In all honesty, you're the first woman to pick me up – and I've been in this biz for ten years."

Sarah knelt down and reclined on the bed, rolling onto her back. She placed her feet flat on the surface then teasingly parted her legs, allowing the woman to see between.

"You think I've ever done this either?" Sarah replied, presenting herself almost like she was at the gynecologist, the lamp light bathing her.

The woman was in her late thirties, but looked good, her body athletic and she had long muscular legs and a firm chest, especially as she removed a black leather jacket, and the thin t-shirt underneath revealed the prominence of dark nipples.

"Personally, I ain't been with a woman in almost five years." She confessed.

"Well, you will tonight." Sarah replied, and pulled her slip up over her belly, revealing her tattoo, then began to run two fingers through the trimmed tufts of her blonde pubic hair.

"I'm aching, for a nice slow fuck." She breathed, words that immediately brought the woman over, causing her to climb on the bed, her stunning dark-brown skin glowing in the light as she moved forward, until she planted a kiss firmly on Sarah's mouth.

Sarah gasped. She lay in bed and could see the lamp above shining down on her. Had she been dreaming? It felt so real. Slowly she sat up to find herself alone and naked as the covers fell to her waist. She turned and got up, before flinching at feeling something cold and wet as her feet met the floorboards. Looking down, she then grimaced to see a trail of crimson footprints leading toward the bed from an open doorway. The woman, who's name Sarah realised had never been shared, was nowhere to be seen.

Sarah did not understand. She remembered meeting the woman, and arriving at the room, even kissing and making love

– it had been amazing, however out of character for her – then, nothing. Now this … *was that blood?* … *What was going on?*

Sarah got up and walked hesitantly towards the room, slowly raising a hand to push the door, but froze as she discovered more blood staining her skin about her fingers and down her arm. A light coming from within partially lit up her body. Hesitantly, Sarah pushed the door open further, then stepped inside only to find a large pool of blood coating the tiled floor next to a tub. Backing off in horror, she collided with the doorframe. This could not be real, she told herself. *I will wake up and this will all be a dream!*

Plucking up courage, Sarah walked inside to see if her fears would be confirmed. She stepped over the blood; it's crimson surface casting an upside down reflection, and peered into the tub – and to her utter distress – discovered the woman laid out in an awkward rag-doll fashion, totally naked and with her throat cut. Blood splashed the interior and sides of the tub heavily, and a crimson handprint was smeared across the wallpaper.

Suddenly a memory flashed in Sarah's head – she had watched the woman leave her side and walk into the bathroom to freshen up. She remembered going over to the woman's bag on a cupboard beside the door, and routing through it, then finding a switchblade, which she opened, seeing the serrated blade glint in the dull light.

She had murdered her. She knew she had murdered her, and even remembered not having the slightest issue with it – at the time. Yet now, oh God – she had murdered someone! What was she going to do? If anyone found out she would be locked up for certain. She had never done anything even remotely violent before – but now she had just attacked a woman and cut her throat, to the point of even taking pleasure in it.

Sarah collapsed onto her knees, overwhelmed as she began to tremble with both fear and panic. This could not be happening, but deep down she really knew it was, she knew what she had done, and it was a feeling that nobody should ever experience. Everything around her began to crumble, her life, her fiancé, her job – none of it mattered anymore because she had just taken someone's life – and there was no way of excusing herself.

Gradually she calmed, and ran a shaky hand over her face, leaving a red smear as she did so, even though she did not realise. She just stayed there, sitting haphazardly on the floor up against the bathroom doorway. She began to feel that it was over – she was done. Nothing could take away any of it, nothing could un-do it. Her life was finished. Simple as that.

But did it need to be? She eventually asked herself. She had killed a prostitute – nobody was about to miss her. She understood that much. If somehow, she could hide the body, perhaps - just perhaps, someone would think she had gone away – and anyway, didn't hookers get killed or whatever all the time? It wasn't all that unusual in such a line of work. Just ask Gary Ridgeway.

A newfound confidence began to develop within her. She got up from the floor and returned to the bedroom. White sheets were strewn across the mattress as evidence of their passionate encounter, and suddenly Sarah snatched them away, gathering them up, before carrying them to the bathroom.

Inside, she dropped the sheets in a ball on top of the toilet, then ran the taps on the tub to wash the blood from the woman's naked skin and drain it away down the plug hole. Grabbing some towels from a shelf, she went down on hands and knees, and dabbed at the floor to soak up the thick pool of blood – certainly no easy task.

Eventually, almost half an hour later Sarah stood heavily stained in blood, still naked, but the bathroom was spotless. The woman's body lay on the floor, concealed within the sheets that were secured at both ends. Sarah sighed – she had done well, as she climbed into the tub and ran the shower, finally washing herself, grabbing a sponge to slowly soap her body. It felt crazy, unreal and totally at odds with how she had thought of herself up to now – but she couldn't take back what she had done, and at least this way she had a hope of coming out of it unscathed. *All I gotta do now,* she thought, *is dispose of the body.*

VIII

Darren had gathered information from a couple of prostitutes who worked the same area as the person he had been trawling the streets for. Heading further into the city, it was getting late, the night turning out cold and bringing with it a light rain fall.

Reaching the more built-up suburbs and housing blocks, his headlights caught a figure staggering in and out of the road, walking rather drunkenly. As he drew closer, his eyes widened in disbelief as he recognised a woman, walking towards the car. He slowed to a halt just as she collapsed against the car's bonnet. Quickly he climbed out, rushing over and then noticed blood and her state of undress. He grabbed her and she looked to him as he took her in his arms, and she collapsed against him.

"Lisa! It's me! What happened?"

The woman lifted her head to look at him again, more blood staining her face … she appeared catatonic.

"Come on, let's get you home." He added, walking her around to the passenger side, opening the door and helped her into the car.

Sitting alongside her, he looked to her as she lay slumped in the passenger seat, slightly breathless, her chest heaving beneath the jacket. Blood stained his seat and the surrounding upholstery. He was hating the thoughts in his head.

"Who did this to you? Lisa…" He said quietly, as if scared of the answer.

She murmured like she was only semi-conscious, then said: "It's ok, it's not my blood… just, just drive."

Darren adjusted the gear stick then trod down on the accelerator, heading into the night.

Opening his eyes, Darren lay in bed trembling, the realness of the dream brought back painful memories. He brought a hand up from beneath the sheets to wipe some sweat from his brow, then realised how the satin was clinging to his body. Slowly he rolled over onto his back, sighing loudly. He thought he had put such memories behind him. Why was he thinking about her now, after all this time? Surely, that part of his life had been gone long enough for it to not still be a part of him. Darren didn't know how he felt – was he scared or nostalgic?

He sat up, suddenly jolting at finding the bedroom door wide open. Standing in the doorway, silhouetted by the outer light was a lone figure. Darren rubbed his eyes to confirm he was not still dreaming, and then leaned forward for a better look.

"Lisa?" He whispered at a barely audible level.

Slowly the figure walked into the room, and Darren sighed with relief to see Sarah, still in her flimsy slip. She looked to him as she reached her side of the bed. For a moment, he just stared at her, comforted by her presence.

"Where have you been?" He asked quietly.

Sarah then climbed onto the bed and noticed how his body glistened and the sheets had turned near-transparent against his legs.

"Hey, you OK? You're dripping wet!" She remarked, running a hand backwards across his brow, "And you're hot as hell."

Darren embraced her, the musky scent of long dried perfume all that he needed.

"I just had a bad dream. That's all."

Sarah put her arms around him as his head rested against her breast, and she began to stroke his hair.

"Was it scary?" She asked, eyes wide, looking around the room.

"Yeah a bit." He replied, then wrinkled his brow, "Your heart's racing." He added.

Sarah looked worried, "Oh… erm, is it? I killed a bug just now. A big bug."

Darren breathed calmly, "Hmm… and they said this apartment was free of that kinda thing. Figures…"

Sarah forced a smile, holding him tightly.

Friday 25 July

Following morning, Patricia was standing in her room, dressed in a cream trouser suit, and had decided to leave her hair down. She approached a dressing table and sat down, then raised her round spectacles to her face and put them on. She hadn't ever really needed glasses, but she did think they made her look more sophisticated. As she went to lower both arms, she noticed the bandages.

Gently she pushed one sleeve back, and the bandage to her left wrist hung loose…dry blood still discoloured the material. Patricia had almost forgotten what happened – what with everything else that had occurred, and quickly unravelled the gauze to lay eyes on her wound afresh. Her mouth dropped open with disbelief to find no cut or scar. Her wrist was perfect, unblemished – like it had never happened. Quickly she unwrapped the gauze from her other wrist to discover exactly the same – both cuts had vanished.

A knock then came to her door. She glanced over her shoulder, and the door opened. Darren poked his head in.

"You ready? David wants us at the Hotel for 9:30." He said.

Patricia was looking wide-eyed at him – then he noticed the unravelled bandages on the dressing table.

"Hey, what you doing?" He asked accusingly, and entered, coming up close beside her.

"Darren, look!" Patricia then remarked and held up both hands.

Darren was amazed.

They arrived outside a Hotel on *South Biscayne Boulevard* that had been closed for the last two days. Yellow Police tape closed off the tall wide entrance doors and a Police squad car was visible parked in an alley beside the building.

"How did David manage to swing this?" Patricia asked.

Darren shut off the engine, looking to the hotel with intrigue.

"He has a brother who is kinda high up in the FBI." He answered.

"I guess that comes in useful."

"Well, you'd think so, yes. However, David's brother is a bit of an asshole. He went for dinner last night at some swanky restaurant just to bring the guy around."

"Well, I'm sure he has to cover his back." Patricia added.

They entered the Hotel through the front, and a Police officer approached as soon as he saw them. He stared at Darren sternly, then eyed Patricia up and down.

"I'm sure you know this place is currently off limits to the public." He said.

Darren opened his mouth to speak, but was prevented from doing so as David appeared.

"It's OK officer, they're with me." He said.

Patricia smiled at David, happy to see him. He had been so kind to her the last time they had spoke, she really wanted to get to know him more.

"So, we gonna take a look at this thing or what?" Darren said.

David and Patricia made eye contact briefly, then David looked at Darren.

"Follow me." He said.

Meanwhile at Boomer, Burns & Brunt law firm, Sarah followed three well-dressed men into a boardroom complete with a long table in the centre. She stood beside a large man in his sixties with grey hair and a neatly groomed beard. Two slightly younger men sat down opposite, the one placing a brief case on the table and opening it. The large man standing with Sarah was *Montgomery Brunt*, one of the partners and a respected attorney. The man with the briefcase was an attorney from another firm, and the gentleman sitting with him, in his early fifties was a client, *Jeremy Valmont*.

Montgomery took a seat and ignited a fat cigar.

"This case has been drawn out long enough. The court date is scheduled for next week. What are we looking at here, gentlemen?" He began, puffing smoke into the air around him.

Sarah stood silently. She wasn't feeling up to any of it, her mind understandably elsewhere. She was nervous, paranoid and butterflies were playing merry hell with her stomach. Hopefully none of it showed.

"My client, Mr Valmont is also keen to settle this matter. Your client has a very weak case for custody, and I have to say does not fare well against my client's strong respectability." The other attorney replied.

"Well, we also have the matter of the events leading up to our client's current problems." Montgomery interrupted, "We do not think taking his son off him indefinitely will be of any help … if anything it may only sink him further."

Jeremy Valmont sighed loudly, "If I may speak up, sirs. This is a very delicate matter. Mrs Valmont and I have both been through a lot of emotional stress. We love our grandchild very much, and only think that subjecting him to any more time in the custody of *Benjamin* is only going to prove detrimental to his future. He is at a very influential age, and that is not a start my wife, or I want for him."

Montgomery dabbed some ash off the end of his cigar and placed it down in an ashtray. As he looked to the two men, Sarah's eyes bulged as she began to feel his hand move up the back of her leg and under her skirt, to caress her inner thigh. She closed her mouth firmly to stop herself from gasping.

"Sarah…" He then said, and she jolted, looking down at him, "I want you to tell these men what you have done."

Sarah frowned, "Excuse me?" She remarked.

She had been paying little attention. Montgomery slowly moved his hand from under her skirt, and looked up at her, "I said, please will you tell these men what you have done."

"But sir…" She replied nervously – *surely he couldn't mean…*

"Are you stupid, young lady? The work I asked you to prepare for this meeting. You have it with you, don't you?"

Sarah's heart went into her mouth. She had left the documents at Darren's apartment, having felt so painfully lost and bewildered at the thought of facing work.

"It's er... not finished, Sir." She confessed nervously.

Montgomery looked furious. He glanced to the men who stared at him mockingly.

"This meeting is adjourned. We will make further arrangements soon, I promise." He said, then got up.

"This is unacceptable, Mr Brunt. We have both had to make vast changes in our schedules to be here today. How long is this going to take?"

"I'm sure Miss Hartshorne here has everything in hand." He said, and Sarah forced a smile as the other lawyer got up, followed by Jeremy Valmont, and they followed her out of the room.

Eventually Montgomery walked into an office with Sarah, then turned and slammed the door shut. She jolted in fear as she stood by his desk, feeling ashamed.

"I'm really sorry, sir." She said.

He looked at her, "Do you realise what you have done? You stupid girl ... this was a very important meeting, and you have just fucked the whole thing right up!! What am I going to say to these people now?"

Sarah looked down at her feet, wanting to crawl under a rock.

Montgomery then approached her. She could smell his aftershave. His hand nudged her chin, raising it so she looked him in the eyes.

"I should fire you." He then said quietly.

"Please… don't do that." She replied.

Montgomery noticed a tear in her eye, and raised his stubby finger to catch it just as it released. Raising his finger to his mouth, he savored the taste.

"No need to cry. I'm sure there's something you can do to make this better."

Sarah looked at him, and instantly knew what he wanted. He began to unfasten his trousers, and she dropped submissively to her knees.

IX

Patricia placed a hand over her mouth as nausea engulfed her, "God, I don't feel well."

David glanced to her as Darren lingered by the open door in the hotel room where twelve women had lost their lives. A stale odour lingered. In the centre of the room was a long sofa that curved into an 'L' shape, and it had been wrapped in plastic, but still large crimson stains soaked the otherwise creamy-white fabric.

"You OK, Patricia?" David asked in reply, watching as Patricia backed off to reveal a large burnt-into-the-carpet outline of a figure.

"Do you recall what that poor girl said about this?" She asked, before crouching down, bringing a latex-gloved hand forward to touch singed fibres.

"Yes. She said that it was 'her' … whatever that meant."

"Do you have any belief in the supernatural, David?" Patricia asked, not shifting her eyes from her view of the macabre image.

Darren then stepped forward, "Aren't we supposed to be taking photographs or dustin' for prints?" He interrupted.

David looked over to him, "We're not allowed, mate. Just standing here is almost risking my brother's job. Let's just look around."

Darren looked down at Patricia, who seemed transfixed, then followed David to an adjoining room. Patricia brushed her hand over the carpet again.

Inside a large bathroom where a jacuzzi was sunk into a marble floor, David glanced around to see carved writing on the walls.

"It's Latin." He confirmed.

"How'd you know? Can you speak it?" Darren asked.

"Some."

"What does it say?"

"Well, it's not written in any way I have seen before. It's confused, meaningless."

"Can you make anything out?"

"Just a few words … listen." David replied, and stood by the wall to read, "Our lord of judgement, bring forth thy tortured soul …"

"Fuck. What's that supposed to mean?" Darren remarked.

"Your guess is as good as mine."

Then they heard Patricia call from the other room.

"Hey, guys…"

Darren and David returned to the room and saw Patricia one end of the sofa.

"Give us a hand moving this thing, will you?" She asked.

"Why the hell for?" Darren replied.

"I think we got something."

David sighed, then walked the other end of the sofa, and together with Darren's help, they were able to lift and carry it a few feet to one side – revealing, to all their considerable surprise – a huge heart-shaped logo, with the words 'Darren & Lisa forever' – written in blood.

Darren stepped back in amazement and shock.

"Who's Darren & Lisa? The victims were all female." David announced.

Patricia gave an inquisitive look to Darren. He focused on her face uncomfortably, then David glanced at both of them.

"Am I missing something here? Do you guys know what this message means?" He asked.

Darren was silent. David looked to Patricia. Darren then spoke up.

"No. It means nothing to me." He said, then turned and walked out of the room.

David followed after him, but Patricia was quick to rush forward and grab David by the arm.

"Let me speak to him." She said, then hurried out.

Patricia followed after Darren as he walked swiftly down an outer corridor.

"Wait up – what was that all about – aren't we all in this together?" She said.

Darren paused, then looked at her, his face a picture of uncertainty and abject fear.

"The last time anything like this happened to me, I was nearly destroyed."

"What do you mean?" Patricia asked.

"I'm not going into it now, not with you. But this is fuckin' messed up - and with what's been happening with you, those cuts just disappearing, you gotta realise there's forces at work here we can never hope to understand." Darren replied.

"That's not you talking, Darren." - Patricia then lowered her voice to just over a whisper, "We have stumbled on this thing. We're all over it now. To just turn your back would be cowardly, and you are no coward."

Darren stared at her sternly, "Aren't I?"

At the Law firm, Sarah was in a room, and ran a tissue across her lips. She loathed the taste, maybe it was his diet as it was much worse than Darren's – but either way, it refused to shift from inside her mouth. A knock came to a door, and at first she just remained silent. There was a sofa in one corner, where a discarded tie was slung. It was *his* tie, and it was probably him now looking for it. She rushed over, grabbed it then returned to the door, turning the doorknob slowly before opening it wide.

She gasped to see a black woman, a little older than herself. Her name was Vanessa, and she was a friend, of sorts. Sarah was sure she knew what Mr Brunt liked to do, but it had never come up in conversation. She guessed Vanessa may be in a similar position. It wasn't exactly something you could chat and laugh about afterwards. Yet it had kept them both in well-paid jobs – *so, that was OK, right?*

"Blake is here to collect you. You finish at twelve, yeah?" Vanessa said, a little too much lipstick as usual.

"Blake?" Sarah replied, not really listening.

"Your fiancée – remember?"

Sarah then smiled, "Blake, yeah, sorry. I kinda had a late night. It's been a rough week."

"Wanna talk about it?"

Sarah stared at her, so wanting to have a shoulder to cry on, but nobody was ever really going to understand, especially when she did not understand it herself.

"Thanks, but no. I think I just need to go home." She answered.

Soon Sarah was seated in the passenger seat of Darren's car, as they drove through busy traffic, everyone in a hurry to go to lunch, it seemed.

"You left early this morning, didn't even say goodbye." He remarked.

"I had to be at work. Can we take straight off back to yours? I left some stuff there. I should probably get it back to the office this afternoon sometime." Sarah said.

"Well, yeah, of course. I want something to eat though. How about lunch?"

Sarah was looking out of the window, and didn't reply.

"Lunch sounds good." Darren answered for her, and then drove by the wine bar to see two Police squad cars and an ambulance.

"Hello ... what's gone down here?" He announced.

Sarah suddenly looked horrified as Darren slowed the car down, and she saw a body bag get thrown into the back of a coroner's van. The entire colour rapidly drained from her face.

"Hey, let's go to that place, you know, the one that does those great salads." She suddenly enthused, turning to look at Darren.

"Shit. Looks like something has happened – man, even this place is going to the dogs now."

"Can we just go? I don't need this right now!" Sarah snapped.

As they began to pass one squad car, a well-built black man caught sight of her as he stood with a smaller black man. For a lingering moment, they just stared at one another, until Darren revved his engine and sped away.

"You know that girl?" the smaller black guy asked.

"Face looked familiar. Did you recognise that guy with her? Where have I seen him before?"

"Hey, he's that detective? Lives a couple of blocks from here; Brian ... no. Blake! That's it! Blake Thomas."

"Oh yeah. Thinks he's a fuckin' hot shot."

The bigger black guy then stepped out onto the road and watched Darren's car disappear into the distance.

A door burst open in an office and the big black guy stormed in, reaching a large series of security monitors.

"The cops haven't been in here yet, have they?" He asked, as the smaller guy lingered by the door, then entered slowly.

"Nah man, they're still smokin' the dumpsters out back for prints after *Lelaina* was found. Why?"

"Just something I saw when I was reviewing the footage from last night – disregarded it at the time, but now after this shit…"

The big guy sat down and began to press some buttons and pull switches. Security footage from the previous night came on, showing the tall black prostitute standing outside the rear entrance of the club. People passed her by for a few seconds, then Sarah appeared, wearing very little but for her corduroy jacket, and was chatting with the prostitute. There was no sound, but a time in the corner read: 00:15.

"That's the blonde!" The smaller guy remarked.

"I knew it. She could have been the last person to see Lelaina alive."

"What's a girl like her doing dressed like that at that time of night? She looked kind of up-market just now."

"She's been to the bar a few times. *James* has served her. She's always had this thing, an attitude, like she's better than everyone else."

"Maybe we should tell the cops about this."

"No way! They don't give a damn about some dead hooker. They'll just file it away and forget about it. We're all she has now, and this bitch knows something." The big guy replied sternly.

X

Sarah had not touched her food. They had both ordered salads as anticipated, and Darren was mopping up the mayonnaise and remnants of chopped carrot on his plate with a piece of bread. Her mood hadn't gone unnoticed.

"You alright? Not hungry?" Darren asked, then raised a cappuccino, taking a gulp.

"Why'd you ask?" Sarah answered, not looking up from her plate, "I'm OK … it's just been a hard morning."

"That case still troubling you?"

She did not reply, moving her fork through some coleslaw with no intention of having any.

"Sarah?"

"What?!" She snapped and looked at him.

"Something's up. You've hardly spoken since I collected you."

"Nothing's up. Just drop it, alright?"

Darren relaxed back and looked around the small but elegantly furnished diner. A strong sun was beaming in from a large main window, bathing patrons as they sat at tables, looking like they were having a far better time than he was.

"We went over to the crime scene today. Not a pleasant experience, I can tell you."

Sarah nodded.

"Something bad went down there. None of us know really what we could be stumbling on. There's still so much that remains a mystery."

Sarah pushed her plate away from her and sat looking restless. She glanced around the diner also, and caught sight of a pretty blonde waitress as she served an elderly couple some desserts.

"How about some ice cream?" Darren then asked.

Suddenly, Sarah got up, straightening her suit with a brush of her hands.

"Where you going?"

"I need to go to the bathroom." She replied, then walked away.

Darren watched her leave, then took his wallet out from his jacket.

A few minutes later, Darren entered the outer corridor, looking frustrated. He didn't understand what was going on with Sarah. Obviously, she was having problems at work. He knew how much this Valmont case was bothering her. Yet whenever it came to talking about it, she was a closed book. He wished he could get through to her, make her realise he was there to help.

He reached the door to the ladies bathroom, smiling at a brunette who exited, before looking away to avoid suspicion. Once alone, he slipped into the bathroom and closed the door. Finding himself in a beautiful, pastel-pink room with a series of toilet cubicles and a long mirror before a row of washbasins, he thought to himself, it was probably the nicest public bathroom he had ever been in … not that he'd ever frequented ladies' bathrooms. He felt a little awkward being there, but as he pondered leaving, a faint weeping caught his attention.

Slowly he approached the cubicles, and the weeping became clearer. With a heavy sigh, he tried to think what to say, guessing the sound was coming from his fiancé. In all likelihood, she was probably going to go crazy at him for following her. He reached one cubical where the door was closed, and he tapped gently on the pink-painted wood.

Inside, Sarah was seated on the toilet, and raised her head from her hands. She had not really gone there to urinate, as her skirt was still hanging over her legs and the seat was down. Her face was flushed and her eyelids red from crying.

"Sarah?" came Darren's voice in a gentle tone.

Sarah bowed her head again, then stood up, straightening her clothes, then approached the door. She stopped herself short of opening it, resting her forehead against the wood, and exhaled.

"Are you in there, Sarah?"

A smile slowly formed on her face, and she unlocked the door, then opened it, suddenly pulling Darren inside.

"Hey!" He gasped as the door was closed again and he was thrust against it.

"Don't say a word!" She whispered, then planted a firm kiss on his open mouth, burying her tongue.

Darren was taken back, unable to comprehend what was happening. This was not like Sarah, she was normally so reserved.

Eventually their lips parted, leaving a trail of saliva to hang delicately between them. Darren examined her eyes, an undeniable gleam of lust evident.

"Sarah, I…" He whispered, then she pressed a finger to his lips to silence him.

"What did I say?" She replied, then slowly sank to her knees, quick to unfasten his belt and roll his trousers down to his ankles.

Darren's black briefs bulged to show that despite his shock, elsewhere he had responded.

Sarah grinned up at him, and for the first time since they had been together, he saw her in a new light. She took out his erection and caressed it in both hands as the veins popped. A shadow was cast over her face, brought on by a single fluorescent light shining down on them from the ceiling. She smiled again, taking the head in her mouth, rolling back the foreskin with her lips, then drew in his erection further until his balls met her chin.

Darren watched in amazement. She was holding her breath, deep throating him and not gagging. He had only seen such like in adult movies. This was not the Sarah he had fallen in love with; but he liked it for a whole other reason.

She removed his penis from her mouth, gasping for breath, and chuckled. She then proceeded to feverishly suck him, bobbing her head and taking him in and out of her mouth until the length was slick and dripping ropes of saliva. Darren was transfixed.

After a moment, Sarah stood up, quick to reach under her skirt to tug at her lace panties, dropping them to the floor. They paused, looking at each other, until Darren moved forward, and Sarah placed one foot on the toilet seat, giving him easy access to her as his stiff penis pressed against her belly. Her scent was of sex, her warmth was of sex. It had come unexpected, but it was also exactly what both of them needed right there and then. Darren closed his mouth over hers, kissing her passionately, one hand pressed to the back wall, the other around her waist. The tip of his erection was rubbing deliciously against the growing slickness of her vagina. He had to be inside her – he had to fuck her. Darren thrust against her and she let out a small yelp, then he thrust again, and his penis sank in to the hilt. Darren and Sarah's sex life had always been good. He was quite a horny guy most of the time, and she was mostly eager to please, but she was also a little shy, and the whole idea of having sex like this, not the least in public, was out of the question – until now.

Darren began to fuck her, his lips smearing her lipstick across her face and her perfume fueled his desire. He thrust against her fast and without reservation. She groaned, gyrating her body with him, until the cubical itself began to creak. Sarah moved back and he went with her until she sank onto the toilet seat, and he pressed his hands to the wall, just above her head as she raised her knees, grunting as he began to piston in and out - pumping into her over and over.

As she looked up at him, she could see sweat form on his brow, his muscles bulge through his shirt, and he was gritting his teeth every time it felt too good.

"Come on!" She encouraged, "Do it – you want it don't you? Then fuck me. Fuck me hard!!"

It was another shock. Sarah very rarely swore, but her expletives just made Darren thrust harder, his balls slapping her flesh every time he impaled her, and he knew that moment of no return was closing in on him.

"God. Sarah…." He gasped and pounded her swollen pussy faster and more violently than he had ever done before.

It was a surreal experience, almost like he wasn't fucking his fiancé at all, but someone else, someone from his past, the only time before that he had known sex like it. So savage, so utterly carnal.

Suddenly, her hand pressed against his chest, halting his thrusts, and he stared at her, panting loudly. Her expression had changed. It was no longer a look of lust, but one of shock, despite her ragged breathing.

"No!" She gasped, then beat her fists against his body, "Get off me!!" She yelled.

Darren withdrew, staggering as his erection quickly wilted, leaking semen. Alas, any orgasm had passed him by like a freight train.

"What is it?" He replied, confused.

Sarah felt violated. She did not understand how it had happened – she only recalled crying in the cubical, and not Darren at all. What was he doing invading her privacy?

"Get the fuck outta here you bastard. Get out!!" She shouted, clamping her legs shut in embarrassment.

Darren said no more, turning to the door and opened it, quick to pull his trousers up and fasten them. He was a mess, but he had no time to clean up. He just wanted out – she had made him feel pathetic.

Shortly after, Sarah staggered out of the cubical, her dignity only slightly restored. She had straightened her skirt and tidied her hair from her face, then reached a washbasin and ran the faucet. She splashed her face to freshen herself, then examined her reflection as beads of water dripped from her chin.

"Now just hold on…" She told herself, "…you're alright." She added, standing up straight, then frowned when she noticed something behind her.

Focusing, she stepped aside to reveal the toilet cubical's reflection, and to her utter distress, she saw a black-haired woman, slumped on the toilet, long stocking-clad legs spread wide, a flimsy thong hooked around one foot, and a splatter of semen dripping from her swollen crotch to land in a pool on the tiled floor.

"Of course you're alright." the woman then replied, looking used and spent, "We are one now. Nobody can come between us. We will do what needs to be done to keep it all secret. Our little secret, Sarah."

Sarah was horrified, "What are you? Are you a ghost?" She asked, then looked away from the reflected cubical to re-focus on her own face, and answered herself:

"I am a part of you now. A part that can never be separated. What has been done cannot be undone. Death is only the beginning."

Sarah gasped at her own words, before turning to look back to the cubical again. It was empty.

XI

David's home was a one level beach house with a grand view of Miami Beach. He had decided to take Patricia for a guided tour, his car parked in the long winding driveway alongside two other sporty vehicles. Steps led up to the front, a stylish patio forming the entrance as doors that opened by themselves, greeted them on entrance.

"Wow … this is pretty special." Patricia announced, at first surprised that someone she still considered to be her boss, was now treating her more like a friend, and by the way he smiled and had been looking at her, perhaps something more. It was no secret that she found him attractive, at least no secret to herself; although she couldn't be entirely sure he felt the same.

They entered a large living area with furniture out of a designer's wet dream, where an ordinary TV stood in one corner, but an expensive music centre took up most of the far wall, along side African figurines and a large abstract, modern art painting hung above.

"It's a roof over my head." David replied modestly, removing and discarding his jacket, before approaching a bar.

"Can I fix you a drink?" He asked, stepping behind, then taking out two glasses.

Patricia walked across a black and white zebra-print carpet. It was not exactly to her taste, but it went so well with everything, that she could barely imagine the room without it. She reached a bookshelf on the wall nearest to the music centre and checked out some titles. They all seemed to relate to the paranormal.

"Big X-Files fan?" She asked.

David poured some gin into the first glass.

"Fox Mulder was my hero. If I had ever bothered to go to school, I would probably have got into the FBI like my brother." He replied.

She checked out a row of DVDs and Blu-rays underneath, and raised her eyebrows at discovering they were mostly all pornographic.

"Oh... now that's embarrassing. Not a problem, is it? Kinda hobby of mine."

"I may know some people you might wanna meet." She answered, not the slightest bit offended, that was not her style, and anyway, she liked porn ... some of it at least.

"Come again?"

"You got anything with Justine Emmanuelle?"

"Justine Emmanuelle? Only her entire back cat ... erm, oh, that makes me sound a pervert, doesn't it?"

Patricia walked over to the bar and smiled, "Not at all. We all like sex, don't we? As long as you know, real people don't do it like that." She replied teasingly, giving her most playful smirk.

David was surprised by her words, even though she looked so good saying them. He thought it best to change the subject.

"Well, anyway, can I fix you anything?"

Patricia paused, and rested against the bar, pondering the moment.

"Well?" He asked.

She then stared at him, "Oh, er ... no thanks. Have you got a PC?"

"Yeah, two - an iMac and a laptop. Why?"

"I need to check my e-mail." She replied.

"My office is just through that door. Make yourself at home." He said, gesturing over to a door that stood shut.

Soon she sat before a computer with a large LED monitor, and signed onto her Hotmail. After a brief pause, some messages appeared:

'Dear Patricia,

I just thought I would drop you a line. I've been thinking of you a lot lately. How are things? Still pondering stuff over that mutual friend of ours? What have you decided? If you still need to talk, I'm here for you, I always will be. Things are hectic right now, what with me having so much responsibility lately. I had to let some kid go today. He was slacking off. It was one of the hardest things I have ever had to do. Roll on retirement. Anyway, I'm on Messenger most days. Just keeping my feelers out there. If you have time, sign in and we'll chat,

Harry xxx'

An alert appeared on the task bar of the computer desktop, which said 'Hi.'

It was Harry. Immediately, Patricia launched a Messenger chat and saw Harry's new message appear in a window.

'Are you there? Messenger told me you were online. Can we talk?'

Patricia typed: 'I'm here Harry, and yes, I think we could do with talking. I'm in Miami.'

After a brief pause, Harry's reply appeared: 'Miami? Don't tell me you took up Maitland's offer... did you?'

Patricia glanced around herself to confirm her solitude.

'What can I say. I'm impulsive. Darren is OK... but I need to know more. He has researched a lot about me, and I feel like I hardly know him, even though I'm staying with him at his place.' she typed, 'And there's some weird shit going on here. Stuff that seems linked to his past or something. I can't go on until I feel like we're on equal ground. What ever you know about him, what ever his past involved – I need to know everything.'

A long pause went by. For a moment, she thought she had said too much, and then Harry's reply appeared:

'Give me a few hours to gather a few things together. I'll e-mail you what I've got. I hope it proves helpful'

Patricia smiled, comforted by Harry's kindness, considering their history. Just for a moment, she thought of James, her ex, and how Harry once let him take the fall in a murder case, just 'cause he thought he'd have a shot with her if her boyfriend was out of the picture. *Deluded old bastard.*

'Thank you, Harry.' she typed back.

At Darren's apartment, he approached a door to the bedroom with a mug of coffee. He went to knock, and then paused as he heard Sarah's voice.

"It's OK. He doesn't need to know. Why would he find out?"

Darren's brow wrinkled with concern. Was she making a call? he wondered.

"Never mind any of that now. We've got stuff to plan. If it all works out, nobody will ever be the wiser."

Inside, Sarah was sitting on the bed, a brief case open and some documents spread out before her. She then jolted to a wrap of knuckles to the door.

"Yes?" She answered.

The door opened, and a concerned looking Darren peered in, "Who was that?" He asked.

Sarah looked around, then picked up a cell phone from her briefcase.

"Oh… just my boss. Why?"

Darren entered the room to stand near the bed, the coffee filtering steam into the air. He looked at his fiancé inquisitively.

"Nothing. I made you some coffee."

Sarah lowered the phone, which wasn't even switched on, the bottom missing it's battery pack. She carefully replaced it in the case, gathering together the documents, then sealed it shut.

"Oh, I'm sorry Blake. I have to get right back. Mr Brunt needs this stuff right away." She replied, then got up from the bed, taking her briefcase with her, and walked past Darren to the door.

As she ventured into the hall, Darren followed after her, and reached out to touch her arm, "Hey, wait a minute."

Sarah froze, before slowly turning to reveal a stern expression, "What is it? I'm already running late. Brunt will have my ass."

"It's just… earlier on, at the diner…"

Sarah looked at him, her face relaxing as she smirked, bringing a hand up to brush his cheek, "It just wasn't the right moment. I still love you, baby." She replied, and lay a kiss on his lips, a cold, unfeeling kiss, and she turned, hurrying to the front door.

Darren just watched as she left without saying another word.

Back at the beach house, Patricia returned to the large living room, to see David sitting on a leather sofa before the TV, watching some news. The headlines were detailing the prostitute's murder, with footage of the wine-bar.

"What you looking at?" Patricia asked, and reached the back of the sofa, then half sat on it, her thigh inches from David's neck and shoulders. He glanced up, initially taken back by her proximity, perfume drifting under his nose.

"Er, it's, er… some girl has been murdered … a hooker, above that bar on Westmore Boulevard. Some garbage collectors found her body in a dumpster." He answered.

Patricia glanced to the screen, and leaned closer, until the hem of her jacket brushed the top of his head. He looked up again, and noticed how her breasts strained the buttons of her blouse. He tried not to stare.

The news program ended, and David switched the TV off with a handset. He got up, feeling slightly uncomfortable, then walked away, before glancing back. God, she smells good, he thought.

"So, David…" Patricia said, a finger playing suggestively with the ripple of soft leather on the back of the sofa, "Tell me about yourself."

David stared at her, "What do you want to know?" He replied.

"Where you grew up, what your folks were like, what was your favourite flavour of ice cream, who did you have a crush on in high school – something like that."

David smiled, walking back to the TV, and picked up a DVD copy of Magnum Force with Clint Eastwood. He wasn't looking at it though, suddenly feeling on edge.

"Surely you have a story to tell, a young entrepreneur like yourself." Patricia added, then as he looked back, she swung her long trousered legs over the sofa and sank down to sit on it proper.

"They say that, don't they?" He answered, "Everybody's got a story to tell. I don't think that's me though. I believe you should never really know anyone - because, if you did, what's there to discover along the way? Maybe you and I will learn a great deal about each other someday … but isn't it more exciting to find it out a bit at a time? I was born in Brisbane, Australia. I've got money; I built the agency from the ground up. I have the entire boxset of The X-Files. Let's leave it at that for now, eh?"

Patricia sat with one leg crossed over the other, her high heeled shoe, half hanging off her foot as it rocked to and fro. She smiled attractively, then got up, walking over to the door.

"Let's do that. Now, are we done here?" She replied.

David stared at her for a moment, feeling like he'd said something wrong but chose not to pursue it, grabbing his jacket off a Lazy-boy armchair, "Yeah. We're done. Did you check your e-mail?" He asked, following her as she opened the door.

"I did." She replied, and exited.

XII

Saturday 26 July

The following morning, Darren awoke to a melody playing that resembled 'Help' by The Beatles. He was alone in bed, and a bottle of Whisky lay empty on the floor below. Slowly he rolled over, reaching an arm out, and his hand scurried around the small cupboard top until he found his cell phone. In a slurred tone, he answered 'Hello?' – his head was banging.

"Blake? Do you know what time it is?" came David's voice.

Darren glanced to his wristwatch, hanging unfastened around his wrist. It read: 11:15 a.m.

"Why? What's the problem?" He replied.

"What's the problem? I tried calling you all last night. I left dozens of messages and two texts. The Police have finished with the agency – its work as usual, buddy."

Darren sighed, slowly sitting up, his chest bare.

"I was in all morning. Had a rough night. My head is fuckin' splittin'."

"What are you doing going out when we're knee-deep in shit over that dead girl? Her parents have been bombarding the office all morning with calls. They need some answers, mate – or we're looking at a lawsuit."

"There's not gonna be no lawsuit, David. Nobody knows what happened – at least, not in a way they can explain. We're clean. If we're lucky, this will all blow over in a month or two."

He heard David sigh.

"Give me a couple of hours. I'm a wreck. Things aren't going too good between Sarah and I."

"Oh? I thought you two were crazy for each other. You had a fight?"

"Maybe it's that case she's involved in. She's all over the place right now. She's been acting weird. Last night I was sure she was talking on the phone to someone. She's not been herself at all."

"Shit man. You don't think she's…"

"I don't know what to fuckin' think. I tried calling her, but her phone just rang out. She did say she had a lot on at work, so maybe she was working late. I just, I don't know… I just need to speak to her."

"Well, have you said any of this to Patricia?"

"No. I wanted to, but, well, she's so into being a part of the agency right now, and just talks about the case … and about you. I didn't want to bother her with my problems."

"She's a friend though, yeah?"

"I'd say so, yes. She's playing a lot of this on instinct though, I guess. Her and I weren't that close back home. She's trusting me to make things work."

"Some of the work is on her shoulders too, right? It's not all you." David added, "So, I guess I'll see you later, yeah? Talk to Sarah, man… get this thing cleared up. It's probably nothing."

Darren smiled. David was a good listener, and over the last few months, had become a valued friend. He pulled the covers away and climbed out of bed, then walked, wearing black briefs, over to the bedroom door and opened it. He could hear a shower running.

"I'll do that, David. I gotta go now. I'll tell Patricia to drop by in the meantime."

He lowered the phone and switched it off, then heard the shower stop, and closed the door until only a gap remained. He waited, watching the bathroom door, then bit his lip at the sight of Patricia as she walked out, just wearing a towel, her skin glistening and her wet hair was combed back over her head.

At the law firm, Sarah sat in an office typing. She paused as the door open in front, and Montgomery Brunt walked in.

"Sarah, have you finished that letter?" He asked.

"Ah yes, Mr Brunt." She replied, and took a finished page from a filing tray on the desk next to her laptop.

Montgomery snatched it off her and proofread it as she continued to type. After a moment, he raised his head to look at her.

"This is very good. Hopefully we'll be able to repair any damage your poor conduct up until now might have caused."

Sarah just continued to type, not looking at him. Montgomery approached the front of the desk, and leaned against it, peering down at her.

"Have you booked any time off?" He asked.

Sarah stopped typing and looked at him, "Yes. I was thinking of taking Monday off… could do with some time at home to prepare."

"That sounds like a good idea. Anyway, I was hoping that we…"

"I've been meaning to speak to you, sir – about the other day. I still, well I feel responsible. I think I'd like to make things up to you."

Montgomery frowned, "How do you mean?"

"I know a hotel, a few miles from here. We should spend a night together. Would that be a good way of making things right?"

"I was going to suggest something along those lines myself. I'd like that very much, Sarah." He replied, and leaned forward to stroke her hair back over her left ear.

"Let's say tomorrow night then. There's no need to rush into this, Sir. We both need time to make alternative arrangements."

Montgomery was surprised at how easily she seemed to be going along with his plans, almost making him suspicious. With a concluding smile, he turned away and walked back out. Sarah smiled, and carried on typing, seemingly unaware of the fact she was typing the same sentence over and over and over:

'Get him alone and kill him. Get him alone and kill him. Get him alone and kill him. Get him alone….'

*

That afternoon, Patricia dressed in a blouse, a flowing knee length skirt and heels entered an office at the detective agency, and walked around a desk, taking a seat before a PC. She grabbed the cordless mouse with one hand and it fired up the monitor, and the company's logo was displayed. A name below read: 'H&T Investigations'. She proceeded to sign into her Hotmail account.

Outside in a corridor, David met up with another detective, a black man in his forties.

"So, you heard any more from the Police department?" the man asked.

"No. And I don't want to either. Blake is at home when he should be here, and I'm up to my eyeballs in red tape just trying to keep this place from getting sued."

"It wasn't anyone's fault, David. We all know that. If they thought we had any kind of responsibility for that poor girl's death, they would have closed us down in a nano second."

David nodded, then walked by, reaching the office door, and opened it. Patricia glanced up from the computer screen as he entered.

"So you spoken to Blake?" He asked.

"I saw him briefly an hour or so ago – he was a little hung over."

"Was he out last night? He mentioned to me when we spoke on the phone that he and Sarah are going through some problems."

"They are? I wasn't aware. What did he say, exactly?"

"It's not important right now. Do you want to talk over the case?"

"Ok. I do have something to tell you, David. Will you sit down?"

David stared at Patricia in concern, then took a seat on a sofa by the wall, relaxing back, "Go ahead."

"Since I got here, I've been experiencing nightmares and, well, a few hallucinations." – she chose not to mention her 'incident', "I've been seeing this girl, in her twenties I'd guess, who has been trying to tell me things, but not anything she has said has made much sense. She seemed drawn to Blake and Sarah for some reason."

David slowly sat forward, "When did you last see this 'girl' you speak of?" He asked.

"It's been a couple of nights now. I saw her in my room at the apartment, and she was saying stuff about Blake… but it wasn't clear what she wanted or who she might be."

David bowed his head, "Did she give you a name?"

"She said her name was Lisa."

David suddenly looked at Patricia, and he recalled the message written on the floor of the hotel room where the twelve people were found dead.

"*Darren and Lisa forever*. You think that message is somehow linked to the girl you've been seeing?"

"I don't know, but… I'm starting to believe so."

David got up, walking over to her, and saw her Hotmail inbox on the screen. She looked at it and saw a new message from Harry appear, sandwiched between a Victoria's Secret email and one from her bank.

"I've contacted a friend of mine from New York, someone who knew Blake before all this, better than I really know him." She announced, then clicked on the new mail.

It took a little while to load, and then a message read:

'I've managed to rustle up some case history on our mutual friend. Do not worry; I have kept his name out of it, in case of prying eyes. Open the attached zip folder, and print out what I've sent you.'

Patricia looked up to David, who was staring at the screen with interest. She then opened the file, and a newspaper article, dated six years previous, was loaded up. David leaned closer, and saw a picture of a brown-haired Darren, trying to hide his face with his hand to the camera.

"Is that Blake?" He said, glancing to Patricia.

"He's changed a lot since he lived in New York, I'd say." She replied.

David proceeded to read the article:

'Police Detective turned Private Eye ▮▮▮▮▮▮▮▮ was last night questioned in connection with a series of murders in Manhattan and the surrounding boroughs. A prostitute by the name of *Lisa Ann Watts* was killed following a violent incident at Brooklyn Hospital where she was being detained in relation to the same series of murders. Over the course of one week, four people; one female the others male, were found slain in believed satanic rituals, where symbolic pentagrams were painted in blood on their bodies. So far Police have refused to comment on why Detective ▮▮▮▮▮ was detained, and a full investigation is currently underway.'

David stood up straight and ran his hand back over his scalp.

"Seems like Blake has been through some shit in his past. I knew he had been involved in a few high-profile cases, and seen a lot – but this…"

"Shall I print off the entire document?" Patricia asked.

"I think you better had." David replied.

XIII

At a hardware store in the city, Sarah left a check out, carrying a long case, complete with a small handle. The chubby, middle-aged woman seated at the cash register watched her curiously as she walked out of the store to a jeep parked directly outside.

Sarah placed the case on the back seat, walking around to the driver's side, then climbed in, the engine left running and the radio playing an advert for insurance. For a second, she caught her reflection in the rear-view mirror and smiled whimsically at herself.

Some distance away across the road, was a large pick-up truck, and seated at the wheel was the owner of the wine bar, a man called Andy Wilson. He and his brother had run the bar for a couple of years, and it was generally a good money maker, something Andy was willing to protect no matter what. Starting up the truck's engine, he watched Sarah's jeep pull away, and followed, remaining several cars behind.

Eventually Sarah stopped at a gas station, and pulled up to one of the pumps. Climbing out, a young Spanish boy approached to fill her up, and she nodded to him before proceeding towards the shop.

Inside, she walked along the isle, running her fingers playfully across bottles of wine and confectionaries. She grabbed a big back of potato chips and two bottles of soda, before walking back to the counter. She placed them down as the Spanish man behind smiled at her and rang them up. Taking out a purse, Sarah thumbed through some bills, before removing a twenty.

"Get me some smokes with that too, pops. It's been a heavy couple of days." She remarked, as unbeknown to her the pick-up pulled up outside, and the young boy scurried away as Andy climbed out.

Sarah exited the shop a few seconds later to be presented with Andy leaning against her jeep. She frowned before slowly approaching.

"Can I help you, Mr?" She asked; a shopping bag in one hand and her car keys in the other.

"You can indeed, Miss." Andy replied, then Sarah met up with him, not the least bit intimidated by his presence.

"Well?" She added.

Suddenly he revealed a gun and pressed it into her stomach.

"Leave your vehicle here. You're coming with me." He said.

Sarah stared at him, remaining calm, and opened her door, turning away.

"Are you stupid, lady? What you doing?" He remarked sternly.

"Hold on, I just gotta put these away. This isn't going to take long, is it?"

"Excuse me?" – Andy could not believe how she was acting.

Sarah placed the bag inside, briefly eyeing the case in the back seat, then closed the door, locking it with a key fob, before turning back to Andy.

"Shall we?" She said with a smile.

Andy just stared at her, puzzled.

Worry had begun to consume Darren. He was unable to fathom why Sarah had begun acting toward him like he was her lover one minute and her enemy the next. His love for her ran deep, but her behavior was messing with his head.

Leaving his car by the roadside and walking up to the entrance of Boomer Burns & Brunt, he recognised Sarah's work friend *Vanessa* leaving.

"Hey!" He called after her, and she stopped part way down the steps, the shop windows of a building across the road, reflecting in her sunglasses.

"Oh, Blake… Hi." She replied, removing and placing the sunglasses in the breast pocket of her blouse.

"Hiya. Sorry about this. Is Sarah ready? I thought I'd drop by and…"

"Oh, Sarah's left, about half an hour ago. Didn't she tell you?"

Darren looked puzzled, "Erm no. Did she say where she was going?"

"I dunno. Home I'd guess. She wasn't feeling well."

Darren nodded then turned away. Vanessa watched him walk back down the steps to his car and climb in. She liked Darren, albeit only knowing his other name, but had never really got that familiar. She hoped he and Sarah were OK, realising she had not exactly been into her work lately. She had offered her friendship, but Sarah did not appear interested, in her, Darren or much of anything lately.

Patricia got up from behind the desk in Darren's office at the agency and walked out into the corridor. She could hear voices of clients and the other detectives in the main foyer, but chose not to join them as she headed for David's door. Inside, David reclined in his leather chair behind his own desk, whilst reading the printed-out document detailing Darren's history. The door opened and Patricia entered, making him look up.

"Why is his name blanked out? Is it due to the legal case surrounding the murders?"

Patricia stared at him, knowing David was a little too inquisitive for her not to feel what she was doing could be risky.

"I guess so. My friend didn't want to draw too much attention to Blake. It's in the past now. I think the more important stuff is the killings themselves."

She reached the desk, watching David cautiously, having only let him know what she thought would help.

"He was involved with this hooker then?" David asked.

"Kind of. Lisa Ann Watts. Her brother, Joseph died shortly after, having been in a coma. He had a girlfriend who was believed to be involved in all kinds of shit, including Satanism."

"Sounds like Blake never knew what he was getting into by taking her in. How long ago did you say this was?"

"Six years, more or less."

"I think we need to talk to Blake face to face. He should never have kept this to himself." David said, tossing the document into a filing tray.

He got up, grabbing a coat off a stand in the corner.

"I think I'll drop by the apartment and see if he wants to talk. I'll get something to eat while I'm out. Want anything?"

"I'm easy. Whatever you want, as long as there's meat in it." Patricia answered, then stepped aside as David passed her and left.

*

A short while later, a door opened, and Sarah was thrust into a bedroom. She fell against the bed, and collapsed on her knees. Andy followed her in, looking enraged.

"I don't know what trick you're trying to pull, lady, but you obviously have no fuckin' idea who you are messing with!"

Sarah smirked to herself, crawling up against the side of the bed, before sitting down on the mattress.

"If you are going to rape me, just get it over with." She said, her hair untidy, and one shoe had come off.

Andy paced the floor restlessly, then turned to her.

"I saw you on the camera. You were the last person to see my sister alive. What are you hiding? Why haven't you been to the cops?"

Sarah stared at him with realisation. She recalled seeing his face briefly as Blake slowed down in his car whilst passing by the wine bar, the morning after the prostitute's death.

"You own that bar, don't you? I remember now. Think you're some hot shot, huh? You and your brother think you run this town."

Andy lurched forward to take her face in one hand, pushing her lipstick-coated lips out ridiculously.

"Quit being so fuckin' easy with this, bitch! Who did it? You must have seen something. Who killed Lelaina?"

Sarah's eyes just looked up at him. She appeared so fragile and innocent. Andy removed his hand, then walked away. He approached a tall full-length mirror on a wardrobe, and examined his reflection, before running a hand back over his face and through his hair, which were just short black tufts on top of his scalp. As he refocused, he stared at the mirror and his brow furrowed. He could see a flickering light behind him, and stepped back a little to see a white figure, seated on the bed, blurred and difficult to make out. The figure slowly stood up, long strands of brilliant white hair cascading down its back, and it began to approach, coming into focus. Andy's eyes widened as he saw a bony, witch-like creature with hoofed feet and long fingernails. It then reached out to him, a thin clawed hand coming up to the back of his neck.

Suddenly he turned around, crying out, and Sarah jolted, seated on the bed, looking no different than seconds ago. Yet Andy was shaken. He just looked at her with horror; barely able to get his words out.

"G-get out of here."

"What?" Sarah replied.

"Get out!!" Andy then yelled, and Sarah got up, backing away to the door.

Andy turned away, looking to the mirror again, and slammed his fist into it, and it shattered into a spider's web.

Sarah left the room, coming to stand by a banister next to a flight of stairs leading down to the floor below. Andy had taken her to some house in the suburbs. She did not understand what he was hoping to achieve, as there was no way she could confess. So, the prostitute was his sister, huh? She hadn't really expected that. Yet she had come too far to let it bother her now. She just had to deal with the situation in hand. She looked down the staircase and slowly reached inside her suit jacket. A switchblade was unsheathed, and it glinted in a shard of sunlight coming in from a window behind her.

Back in the room, Andy was still in shock. What had he seen? Was he hallucinating? He tried to think clearly, and began to regret his actions. What on earth was he thinking?

Suddenly, the door burst open and Sarah ran in with a yell, and sank the knife into Andy's back, right between the shoulder blades. He jerked forward, then turned, lashing out with his hand, and smacked Sarah across the face. She let go of the knife, leaving it imbedded, as she hit the wardrobe, then fell to the floor. Andy retaliated in agony, taking the gun from his belt, and fired it twice. One bullet hit the wardrobe door, but the second hit Sarah in the stomach, and she fell on her side.

For a moment, calm was restored, and Andy reached behind his back to pull the knife out, wincing in pain as he did so. He discarded it as his white t-shirt began to turn red, and he aimed the gun.

"What the fuck are you?" He gasped, seeing Sarah lying in a pool of her own blood. She whimpered, saliva hanging from her bottom lip, then looked up to reveal glowing, yellow pupils.

"Please." She gasped, "Please... kill me."

Andy was stunned. He held the gun with a shaking hand, then slowly saw a smile form on her face. She rolled over and began to crawl away on the floor beside the bed, and Andy just stepped forward, following her.

Sarah jolted as the gun went off, and she felt her body press hard against the floorboards. A bullet had entered her back. Then a further shot made blood spurt out of her mouth as another bullet joined the last, and smoke drifted into the air above. Her eyes went wide, and then her face hit the carpet.

Andy stood over her, panting. He had never killed anyone before. He was unable to comprehend the reality of his actions. Sarah was not moving. Blood soaked the carpet all around. She was dead.

Andy backed off, dropping the gun, and it hit the floor with a weighty thud. He sighed, then looked away, before walking to the door. He glanced out into the hall, hearing something. Quickly he rushed to the top of the stairs, and could see down to the front door. A figure was visible beyond the glass. He checked his watch, having lost track of time, of days in the hopeless search for his sister's killer. He hadn't realised it was his wife's half day – and she was at the door trying to get in. Andy panicked, rushed back into the room, then collided with the bed. He fell on top of it, and tried to lift himself back up, instantly aware of his stab wound. He sat up and looked back to the open door. Gritting his teeth as he got back up, he then stumbled forward and slammed the door.

Down at the bottom of the stairs, a black woman in her twenties came in wearing a tunic, obviously a nurse at the local Hospital. Bags of shopping remained on the doorstep, her face desperate as she called out, having heard the shots.

"Andy?"

Back in the bedroom, Andy turned a lock in the doorknob, leaning against it. He was breathless and could feel himself growing weaker by the second. After a moment he began to breathe normally again, his head pressed against the wood. Opening his eyes, he slowly stood upright. With a lick of his lips, he restored some moisture, before turning around.

He came face to face with Sarah – and she held the switchblade aloft. Andy let out an ear-splitting scream, which was then silenced as Sarah slammed the blade into his mouth.

XIV

Darren's car arrived outside Sarah's suburban house, and he switched off the engine. On exiting, he looked to the house as if seeing it for the first time. It was located in a district known as Coconut Grove, and had become a second home in the time he'd known Sarah. He was just nervous for some reason, as he hurried up the driveway, smiling to a neighbour mowing a lawn a few houses down.

Reaching the front door, situated on the side of the house, he rang the bell and waited. He could see himself reflected in the frosted glass. After a few seconds, he rang again, before reaching into the inside pocket of his jacket. Finally, he revealed a set of keys, and inserted one in the lock, gaining entry.

Inside he walked up the narrow hallway, the door remaining open, and passed a telephone on a small table next to a closet. He entered the living room, where the drapes were only drawn a little way, steeping the room in shadow, and saw that the television was on, playing an old black & white movie. She had been home, he figured.

Returning to the hallway, Darren sprinted up the staircase, a myriad of thoughts popping in his head. The bedroom door burst open and he stopped at the foot of a double bed. As much as it went against what he knew of Sarah as a person, her values, he still expected to see her mid-coitus with some guy. The room however, was untouched.

Eventually he descended the stairs and paused before the open front door. A nagging feeling told him he was missing something, a clue, any hint of where his fiancé might be or why she had begun behaving the way she had to him. Walking back down the hall, he went to pass the phone again, but stopped on seeing a notepad lying open and with something scribbled in biro on it. Picking it up, he read a number followed by the name of a hotel. He went cold.

Quickly he lifted the receiver and dialed the number. A female voice answered.

"All our operators are currently busy. Please hold and you will be connected to a representative as soon as one becomes available. Thank you for choosing The Ambassador Hotel."

Darren slammed the receiver down on the table, and it tumbled to the floor with a clatter. Cursing to himself, he paced up and down, then hurried back upstairs and returned to the bedroom, pushing the door open. Turning to the wardrobe, he opened the doors, only to discover it empty, stripped of Sarah's things. Horrified, he looked around then noticed a brown suitcase peeking out from under the bed. He knelt down, but before he could reach for the handle, he saw Sarah's diary on the bedside cabinet. Quickly he stood up and grabbed it. The book was bound in a thick pink leather and embroidered with a flower design. Yet before Darren could open it, he was stopped by a large metal padlock - with no key in sight. Frustrated, he concealed the diary inside his jacket then rushed back out, down the hallway and stairs, before leaving the house - slamming the door behind him, resulting in a crack to the glass.

At the Agency, Patricia was sat on the edge of Darren's desk, watching a Police report on the TV beside a bookcase, and it was detailing the prostitute's murder again, this time with a few more pieces of evidence. A reporter was standing beside a table with some items on it, and held up a large switchblade. The camera showed a close up of it as the reporter commented.

"Forensic evidence returned by the Police this morning has reported that a knife almost exactly like this one, would have been used in the murder."

Patricia frowned as a thought occurred to her, and got up, walking around the desk. Picking up a file, she opened it to view the printed-out newspaper cuttings. It showed a grainy photo of a body, covered by a sheet from the scene of a murder. She read what was written beneath.

'Travis Matheson, a 23-year-old student was found murdered in the Queens district. A knife thought to be a switchblade with a serrated, razor-sharp edge, is believed to have been used. This connects the murder to the killing of a local musician. Additionally, a pentagram symbol was founded carved into the victim's chest, matching the scenes of up to now, three murders.'

Patricia placed the file to one side, before walking over to a wall on the opposite side of the room, where a large map of Miami was displayed. She examined it closely, then took a pin from the cork-board next to it, and used it to mark the location of the wine bar.

Sarah sat in the back of a cab, her corduroy jacket buttoned restrictively up to her neck. She did not look her best; her face pale and she felt tired.

"So, where's it going to be, lady? I can only drive so far." the Mexican cab driver asked, looking to Sarah via a wonky rear-view mirror where a set of dice hung.

Sarah sat forward, looking to the outside world with curiosity. She was quite a distance from her house and desperately needed a change of clothes. She just prayed Darren was not home.

"2nd Avenue – Coral Gables." She answered, reciting the apartment address, then relaxed back.

*

Shortly afterwards, Sarah let herself into Darren's apartment and called out on entering the hallway.

"Blake? You home?" She said, and when no answer came, she quickly entered the kitchen.

Inside she removed her jacket to reveal a blood-stained blouse complete with one bullet hole just above her waist and two others on the back. She was quick to take it off, leaving just her bra. The skin underneath was also stained, her belly soaked crimson and two fresh bullet wounds were planted either side of her spine. She screwed the blouse up into a ball and stuffed it into the washing machine, then went to switch it on, until a knock came to the door.

Startled, she looked back, and then hurried out. Soon she entered the bedroom, and opened a drawer in a cabinet to find some of her clothes she kept there for when she stayed over, which was becoming less and less a thing.

Eventually she opened the door wearing a black t-shirt and sweatpants, shocked to discover David standing in the outer corridor.

"Oh, Sarah – Hi." He said, equally surprised to see her.

"Yes?" She retorted, monotonously.

David looked behind her, but she narrowed the door to stop him seeing in.

"Is Blake here? I've been trying to call him."

"He had to go out. What's it about?" came Sarah's blunt reply.

"Well, you see, this shit over the case – I guess he's told you…"

"Oh yes, the case… what about it?" Sarah asked, intrigued.

"Well, Patricia and I have been going over a few things, some stuff we need to talk to Blake about. Just tell him it's involving his past – he'll get the idea. Do you know when you're expecting him back?"

Sarah looked puzzled, bowing her head in thought, then looked back up.

"No. He didn't say. But I'll let him know you dropped by."

David smiled, "Thanks. So, you and Blake, you two doing OK?"

Sarah stared at him, "How do you mean?"

"I spoke with Blake first thing. Well, more like mid-morning. He was saying you and he were having problems."

"I don't think that's any of your business, David." Sarah replied, "I'll tell him you were here. I'm closing the door now."

David stepped back as the door was closed in his face, and he glanced around himself, feeling uneasy. Obviously, nothing had been resolved in the short time since he spoke to Darren last.

Sarah walked back down the hallway, mumbling incoherently to herself.

"He thinks I'm stupid. I've seen how he looks at me. He probably wants to fuck me. He's probably looking to split us up. I won't let that happen. Jealous freak. Who does he think he is?"

She was not pleased with David's interest in her and Darren, nor did she like the idea he was delving into his past. She knew what was hidden there, or at least a part of her knew, and it could very easily ruin everything.

XV

As evening drew in, Patricia was handed a glass of wine in David's office. She smiled as they clinked glasses, then she walked slowly over to a sofa, sitting down before taking a sip. An empty carton of sushi stood next to a box of fried chicken on a table nearby, its strong aroma filling the room.

"This whole case is beginning to give me a headache." She confessed.

David approached, then sat down beside her, close enough so she could make out the brand of cologne he was wearing… Dior if she wasn't mistaken. She stared at him long and hard, looking for any hint of mutual attraction in his eyes. There was certainly something, but not enough to be sure.

"Maybe we should be making tracks." He said, and drank a little of his wine.

"What, to go back to the apartment? Maybe Blake needs some time alone, get his head clear."

"Sarah did seem very guarded earlier. Perhaps they just need to talk."

"That's what I meant."

David smiled, lowering his glass, and placed it on a small table next to the sofa, quickly joined by Patricia's. Their eyes met, and for a moment, it was like time froze. Suddenly, Patricia kissed him strong on the lips, and David responded, bringing his hand up to her face, and to her relief, returned her advance with a passion she'd been craving.

Patricia was pushed back until she was reclining on the sofa, and David moved on top of her, their mouths kissing with haste as Patricia tugged at his shirt to free it from the confines of his trousers. David paused, lifting himself up a little. He examined her face with his eyes, and noticed how her lipstick was slightly smeared.

"You sure about this?" He asked.

Patricia nodded, "I want you, David."

David sat up, and removed his shirt in one quick movement, revealing a muscular, hair-less chest. Patricia didn't hesitate and reached forward, unfastening the belt of his trousers, and hurried to unzip him. David watched with anticipation as she released his penis and massaged it as it grew and stiffened in her hand. Ever since he first met Patricia, he had found himself fantasising – he would be crazy not to. Patricia was alluringly sexy, he had thought, and resisting the chance to be with her was the definition of idiocy.

She smiled at him, then moved forward, returning her lips to his and pushing him back against the cushions as she buried her tongue in his mouth. His hand travelled the curve of her back, from her shoulder blades down to her ass, and he drew up the soft material of her skirt to caress her flesh, discovering she was wearing a thong. She was warm to the touch and his erection tingled every time it nudged her thigh – *oh God*, he thought, *I have to fuck her.*

Gradually they moved, never stopping their kiss, and Patricia lay back as his hand grabbed her thong, and yanked it down her legs, until it dangled from one foot and Patricia kicked it off along with her shoe. Her toes pressed against the carpet as her arm wrapped itself around David, and suddenly - he was in her, and she let out a gasp, turning her face away, eyes closed as he continued to kiss and lick her neck. She felt his breathing grow ragged and his movements more forceful, more demanding. It was exactly what they both needed; the tensions of recent events fading away. Patricia sank her teeth into her bottom lip as his penis filled her, hard and thick, and it felt incredible. She couldn't believe how long it had been since she last had sex, especially with a man, and for the briefest of moments she felt more alive than she'd been in years.

David's thrusts picked up pace, full of lust, Patricia equally aroused and responsive. She turned and kissed him, his breath mixing with her own, both of them panting like animals in a torrid struggle, and she clutched her fingers to his ass, urging him on, encouraging, craving - she needed it so badly. Patricia's head raced … she was so very close, and just as soon as she thought she was going to get there, David lifted himself on his arms again, and his erection slipped from her vagina.

Soon, Patricia was straddling him as he sat on the sofa, clothes entirely discarded as their bodies gyrated in a sensual dance, and she began to ride him as they kissed passionately. David held on to her hips as she moved, her ass slapping his thighs. She leaned back, steadying herself with her hands on his knees, fucking herself on his stiffness, and he moved with her, taking a nipple in his mouth and biting on it. She groaned – God this was it, this was what she needed.

Then they were on the floor, and David was over her, thrusting in and out of her slick opening as she yelped, louder with each thrust. She could feel his breath against her neck and his body slid effortlessly against her own, rubbing at her breasts and belly – every part of her on fire. David began to speed up, his movements almost painful, but Patricia was beyond her usual boundaries, she needed release, and he was on his way to giving it to her. Wrapping her legs around him, hooking both feet together, her vice-like grip urged him to continue, as saliva trailed her cheek and he grunted like some untamed creature, his teeth bared.

With a final thrust, impaling Patricia to the hilt, he made this beautiful blonde woman cry out loudly, her orgasm hitting her like a tidal wave, as he emptied himself inside her, his own release combining with hers. David trembled and shook in spasm, then exhaled, collapsing on top of her. Patricia swallowed hard. *Jesus Christ*, she said in her mind, *that was unbelievable.*

Afterwards they lay together on the sofa, naked in each other's arms, and David was stroking Patricia's hair, her head against his chest. The smell of sex had replaced the smell of half-eaten takeout. Raising a glass of wine to his lips, David took a sip, as Patricia dozed. He felt empowered, and deeply relaxed, wanting the moment to last – as all too soon the reality of each other's lives would wake them up from such a dream. Until then, he was willing to wallow for as long as possible.

Darren returned to his apartment and removed his jacket. He entered the living room, taking a packet of cigarettes from his pocket, and unsheathed one, placing it between his lips and igniting the tip with a Zippo. As he walked over to a drink's cabinet, all prepared to drown his sorrows on some expensive wine he had never even corked, he stopped still on noticing red stains on the rug before a marble fireplace. He looked to the Plasma TV for a second, then stepped back, and glanced to the floor again. Further red stains seemed to lead back into the hallway.

Eventually he entered the kitchen and stopped at the washing machine hidden underneath a work surface next to a wash basin. A bloody handprint had been left to dry on the chopping board. His heart went in his mouth.

Rushing back out into the hallway, he checked the front door. There was no sign of forced entry. Confused, he walked back down the hallway and pushed the door open to Patricia's room. The bed had been made and the drapes were open, the patio doors shut and sun flooded the room. He knew Patricia was most likely still out – at least he hoped she was.

Eventually Darren entered the main bedroom and approached the bed. A drawer lay open, and some clothes were discarded to the floor – Sarah's clothes. He placed a hand over his mouth — *had she been back?* He took his cell phone out of his shirt pocket and selected Sarah's name from the drop-down list. It began to ring the other end as he held the phone to his ear.

Meanwhile at Sarah's house, Sarah was standing beside a bed, an open case on the mattress and inside various hardware tools: hack saws, knives and two rolls of duct tape. Her cell buzzed on the dresser, and she turned to snatch it away. She checked the name revealed on the display, then switched it off.

Darren lowered his phone, walking back out of the room, placing the phone on a small table where a landline telephone was based, then returned to the living room. Not knowing what was going on, he slumped, exhausted on the sofa next to where his jacket had been slung. After a moment, he gathered it up in his arms, and reached into the inside pocket.

Taking out Sarah's diary and examining it, he tossed his jacket on the floor, then leaned over to a small cupboard beside the sofa and placed his cigarette in an ashtray. He opened a drawer to reveal a paperknife. He took it and began to work the padlock, then with one swift movement, it broke away, and he placed the knife down on the cushion next to him before sitting back, opening the diary to the last entry – two days previous.

'Thursday 24th July,

Dear Diary

The Valmont case has been really getting to me – it's not that it's that tough a deal, I don't know – maybe I'm just not up to it right now. Blake has seemed distant since his friend has come to stay with us, but I'm not too concerned. I think she is gay anyway. She was watching me, I am sure earlier today. Something weird happened when we tried to talk after about it. Did we kiss? It seems more like a dream now, even though I can still taste her lips. Patricia is a very attractive woman – but what am I saying? Am I getting feelings toward her? Maybe we need to talk – clear the air and try to figure out what went on – if that is, anything went on at all. Since that moment I feel like a different person. Still, I'm staying over again tonight, so any concerns will probably be gone by tomorrow. Oh well – I'll let you know then, I guess. Blake will be home soon – it's getting dark.'

Darren frowned at what he had read – had Patricia come on to his fiancé? He had not even thought of her like that – well, not as a lesbian or whatever she might choose to call it. Yet he also hadn't seen her with any guys, and what relationship he knew of, with some guy called James, had seemed to be off more often than it was on.

He back tracked a couple of entries to Friday, almost a week previous.

'Friday 18th July,

Dear Diary

Mr Brunt touched me again today. That disgusting old pervert thinks he can put his hands wherever he wants, and I'll never do anything. Maybe he's right – I don't want to lose my job, and making a fuss about it would look just as bad on my reputation as his. I don't think it's just me though – Vanessa has had to stay late while I've been allowed to go home. I doubt she's filing his things by how she acts the flowing mornings, like she could die. I promise myself it will never get that way for me, even if I have to find another job.'

Darren felt angry – her boss was placing his hands on her. It made him want to cave the fat bastard's head in. Frustrated, he got up, leaving the diary on the cushion with the paperknife, and returned to the kitchen. He opened the refrigerator, taking out some orange juice. Then returning to the wash basin, he took a tall glass off the draining board, and began to pour some juice, whilst focusing on the handprint again.

As he stared, the juice began to overflow from the glass to soak his shirt sleeve, and he flinched, dropping the glass into the wash basin. His sleeve wet through, he cursed loudly, leaving the carton on the draining board then unbuttoned himself, removing the shirt, and screwed it up, stuffing it into the washing machine. He then froze. Other clothing was already inside. Kneeling down, he opened the machine door wide, then brought his hand back out, and it was covered in blood. He gasped, delving in again, before pulling out to his considerable shock – a blood-stained blouse – Sarah's blouse that he'd got her for her last birthday.

Finally, he stood up; trembling with distress, and raised the blouse to reveal two unmistakable bullet holes, the fabric singed around each entry point.

XVI

Patricia stood in Darren's office by the desk, and scrunched her underwear up in one hand, before concealing it in her handbag. She smiled to herself. Upon waking, that familiar feeling of guilt and shame had hit her, along with the uncertainty of whether or not she'd just messed up her potential career as a Private Eye. Isn't it one of those unwritten rules, to not sleep with the boss? In her still relatively young years, she had also seen too much and done too much to linger on regrets. She chose to think of it as a turning point. Nothing ever happened, she believed, for no reason.

She jolted as she heard David clear his throat to grab her attention. Turning slowly, she saw him in the doorway with his jacket on.

"You off?" She asked, lowering her handbag to her side.

He nodded before approaching. They came together, and he raised his hand to run his fingers back through her hair. Her heart skipped a beat.

"Do you want to come back with me?" He asked quietly.

She shook her head, "Let's not rush things. We have plenty of time. And there's a few things I want to finish off here, then Blake will probably be wondering where I am."

David smiled, understanding despite some disappointment. They kissed slowly, and Patricia closed her eyes in reaction. The feeling he created within her could make her so weak and helpless that when he touched her, she knew she was his without hesitation. Patricia forced herself away and raised her free hand to wipe the taste of him from her lips.

Minutes later, once David had gone, Patricia sat down behind Darren's desk, and opened a printed-out Manhattan map before her. She sighed as she raised a glass of water to her mouth and drank a little, then placed it down again, staring, searching for any kind of meaning to the randomly placed red dots signifying the locations of five people's deaths. With sudden realisation, she grabbed a pen and started to join each dot. As she ran a line from one to the other, her eyes began to widen and eventually she formed the symbol of a five-pointed star: a pentagram.

"Oh..." She remarked to herself.

*

About half an hour later, a cab arrived outside the apartment building, and Patricia paid the driver, before walking up the drive to the front door.

Eventually she exited an elevator and proceeded up the lonely corridor. She let herself into Darren's apartment and closed the door, and went to pass by the living room, until she heard something. It was the unmistakable sound of crying. Slowly she entered to see the living room turned upside down. The drinks cabinet lay smashed on its side, sofa cushions discarded, and there, sitting with his legs hunched up close on the floor the other side of the sofa, was Darren, holding a cushion.

"Darren?" She remarked, rushing over, and dropped to her knees in front of him, "What is it? What's happened?"

Darren just buried his head in the cushion, continuing to weep.

"Hey come on – it's me remember? Tell me what's wrong." She urged.

Darren seemed incapable of words; his sobbing so relentless Patricia could barely stand it. She sighed, reaching forward and took him in her arms, and his head leant against her chest. She patted him on the back, not knowing what to think. It had to be about Sarah. It was the only conclusion.

Meanwhile at David's beach house, he let himself in and walked into the wide living area, discarding his jacket to a sofa, then approached the bar. Pouring himself a Brandy, he took a moment to think. He also didn't regret what had happened. Patricia was a strong personality that he had been immediately drawn to, and as it turned out, was also a fantastic fuck. He was on a high, it seemed, and the strong after taste of the Brandy just added to his good mood. He took another sip from the glass, then turned around, and jolted as the small TV in the corner suddenly came on to a loud scene from a hard-core porn film. It showed a woman with cropped black hair, hands cuffed, a chain dangling from her neck, being double teamed by two burley black guys. It was disturbing, even more for how unexpected it was.

David tore his eyes from it to look across the room, and in the subdued light, took a few seconds to notice someone seated in an armchair the other side of the door. It was Sarah, looking like he had never seen her look before.

"God-dammit! How did you get in here?" He asked.

Sarah smirked, and then muted the aggressive sounds on the DVD. She was wearing a rubber basque, black seamed stockings, high heeled ankle boots, and a black latex thong. She also wore a studded dog collar, her blonde hair tied up on top of her head in a forceful looking ponytail. Bright red lipstick coated her lips, and long gloves ran up her arms to her elbows.

"It pleases you, doesn't it… to see a woman degraded like that, huh?" She commented, "Treated like an animal, a piece of flesh you can violate and fuck with no remorse or any concern for her feelings or her needs."

She slowly sat forward and placed a remote control on a glass table before standing up. David was stunned and found himself backing away to the bar as she approached.

"What the fuck has got into you, Sarah? This isn't you. What's this all about?" He asked.

Sarah smiled, then came up close as his ass met the bar, and he flinched as she raised a gloved hand.

"I am not the person you think I am, David." She said, and David involuntarily squirmed as she ran velvety fingers ticklishly across his cheek.

He closed his eyes. When he opened them again, he let out a gasp, discovering he was once again alone in the room, and the TV was switched off.

Outside parked the other side of the road was Sarah's jeep. She had watched David arrive, and had been waiting, building up courage to make her next move. Without further hesitation she opened the door and climbed out, still dressed in her black t-shirt and sweatpants. She walked across the road, which was free of traffic and the night had grown windy and she sensed there might be a storm on the way.

Back in the beach house, David feeling slightly disturbed, walked over to patio doors and they opened by themselves, allowing him onto a wide balcony with a view of the ocean. Rain began to pitter-patter on the wooden flooring, leaving thick droplets. He remained in the doorway as he raised the Brandy to his lips and finished the dark beverage.

"The ocean is rough tonight, isn't it?" a voice then startled him.

He turned and saw a silhouetted figure standing in the living area behind. It was Sarah, for real this time.

"Excuse me? How did you get in here?"

"Got other things on your mind, David? You left the front doors open."

David did have a lot on his mind. He turned fully and re-entered the room, suddenly recognising Sarah, and lowered his glass.

"What the fuck? Sarah?"

Sarah sighed, glancing around the room.

"You moved this place around since the last time I was here?"

"Not really, but I have a housekeeper who likes to think she can place things wherever she wants … but that's not important. What you doing here, Sarah?"

He was still feeling uneasy after what he supposedly saw.

"I don't know…" She replied quietly, and rubbed her eyes with one hand, "Things aren't very good right now – it's all mixed up."

"Is this about you and Blake?"

"In a way, yes it is. I don't know what's happening, David – I just couldn't face him today. We'd just argue. I thought if I spoke to you, his friend, I could clear something up in my head."

David was concerned, initial worries over her presence fading, and he walked over to a lamp in one corner, switching it on.

"Can I fix you a drink?"

Sarah smiled, but shook her head, "No thanks. Maybe I should go."

"No. It's alright. Talk to me Sarah. I want to help."

Sarah walked over to a long sofa and sat down. David placed his glass on the bar and took a seat opposite in the armchair the earlier vision of Sarah had been seated in.

"Well, I think things haven't been right for a while. Him moving that woman in didn't help, and well, we haven't exactly had a good love life for a while now."

"What is it? Do you feel Blake's too caught up in his work? I know how he can get…"

"I don't know what it is. Maybe it's me. Maybe I've changed for some reason."

"I have spoken to Blake, briefly. He hasn't been involved in the agency because of his concerns over you. He's really upset and self-destructive as a result."

Sarah bowed her head, "These past few nights have been like a dream. I have not felt alive. It's like I have been in some kinda deep sleep, and all I need to do is wake up and it'll all be OK."

"I think you and Blake are worth fighting for. Blake is complicated, I admit, but he loves you."

Sarah nodded, then got up, "Can I use your bathroom?" She asked.

"Sure, it's just out the door, on your right." David replied, pointing a finger.

Soon, Sarah entered the bathroom and switched the light on. She rushed to the washbasin and ran the faucets fully. She had suddenly begun to perspire and breathe heavy. She splashed her face with water, then fixed her hands to the porcelain basin, and stared at her reflection in a mirror.

"No. Not David. He's innocent." She said sternly.

Her reflection then replied: "Why not? Doesn't he already know too much? They are after you, Sarah – and we cannot allow ourselves to ever be caught. He is just another obstacle standing in the way."

"That's not true. David is a good person. He's Blake's best friend."

"The hooker wasn't exactly Charlie Manson either. Her brother had never killed anyone until he thought he could kill us. Their personality is not the issue. We have a task to complete, and David has been chosen."

A knock came to the door.

Sarah forced herself to look away, "Yeah?"

"You OK in there? I thought I heard something."

Sarah did not reply, and looked to the mirror again. Her reflection smiled at her, and suddenly she grabbed a mouthwash cup from a shelf and threw it.

Outside, David heard glass shatter, and in reaction, he opened the bathroom door, to see a tearful Sarah standing before the washbasin, faucets still running, and the mirror on the wall broken, large shards of glass having fallen.

"What happened? Sarah?" He exclaimed.

Sarah placed her hands again on the sides of the basin, her head bowed as she wept.

"You don't understand, David. It's not you, it's not Blake. There are things at work here that have no pity, no remorse. Things inside me, and I feel like I'm slowly losing my identity. I'm losing who I am."

David approached, and brought his hand up to touch her shoulder, "What are you talking about, Sarah? It's getting late. Do you want me to make the guest room up for you? Maybe you should get some sleep."

"Get away from me, David. You don't understand. I've done some terrible things, and if I stay here, I can't be sure it won't happen again."

"Your rambling, Sarah. You're not making any sense." David replied, beginning to feel uneasy.

"No David. I'm making perfect sense. I want to kill, and I can't control the urge anymore."

David frowned, "Excuse me?" He remarked.

Suddenly, Sarah snatched a large shard of glass, turned and slashed David across the chest. He staggered back, falling against the door, and stared in shock. Then he saw Sarah full on - her eyes were glowing yellow. He cried out in horror, and turned, fleeing into the hallway, but Sarah ran after him, colliding with the wall on exit, as David rushed towards the front doors.

Outside, with heavy rain pouring down, the glass in the patio doors exploded as David was thrust out with Sarah clinging to his back, and as he landed on the hard driveway, she sank the shard into his back, blood splashing the tarmac. David screamed in peril, then his head was raised as Sarah grabbed him by the hair, and she brought the shard to his throat, slashing it open with one swift movement.

Shortly afterwards, rain still lashing the ground, Sarah closed the back of the Jeep and walked back towards the beach house carrying a large case. She walked up the driveway, stepping over a partially washed away pool of blood where David's body had been, and re-entered the house.

Inside on the living room floor, where sheets of newspaper were covering the carpet, was David's body. She approached the sofa, and laid the case on top, then released the catches and opened it to reveal various hardware tools; a large hack saw, knives, and two rolls of duct tape.

"Remember Sarah … it's all part of the bigger picture." She then said to herself, and selected a hack saw, holding it up until her face was reflected in the blade.

XVII

Sunday 27th July

Patricia awoke to the sound of a melody playing. She rolled over in her bed and glanced sleepily to an alarm clock Darren had provided her. It glowing red display showed it had just turned ten a.m.

Out in the hallway, Darren exited the kitchen, dressed still in the same clothes from the previous night, looking more than a little wrecked from heavy alcohol consumption and little sleep. The melody playing was his doorbell, and as he shuffled unsteadily towards it, a loud thumping of fists replaced the melody. He reached the door and removed a security chain from the lock before turning the handle. Opening up, he revealed two Police officers standing in the outer corridor.

"Mr Thomas?" the one asked.

Darren stared at them bleary eyed, then nodded.

"Can we come in?" the other officer asked.

"What's this about?" Darren responded.

In the guest bedroom, Patricia had put on a rather short, silk dressing gown her mother had bought her, securing it around her minimal waist with a flimsy rope belt. Eventually she walked out to the hallway and noticed the door standing open ahead of her. Voices could then be heard coming from the kitchen. She ran a hand back through her hair, a little sleep deprived herself having stayed up late with Darren, and walked inside.

Darren was seated at a table as one of the officers sat the other side and his colleague stood the far end of the room, where a number of unattended dishes had been piled.

"So, when was the last time you saw your fiancé, Mr Thomas?"

"I don't understand. Is she in trouble?" Darren replied, as the image of him holding up her blood-stained blouse flashed in his head.

He closed his eyes momentarily.

"Mr Thomas?"

"Officers? What's this about?" Patricia then interrupted.

Darren looked over to her, glad he wasn't alone if any of the fears in his head were about to be confirmed.

"Maybe this would be best discussed down at the precinct."

Darren returned his focus on the officer, "It's been a couple of days. We kinda had a fallin' out. I-I haven't seen her since Friday afternoon."

Patricia observed from the doorway suspiciously.

"Well, Mr Thomas, we have reason to believe that your fiancé, Sarah Hartshorne saw the victims of two recent murders prior to the actual incidents." the officer continued, "We could really do with speaking to her, at least dismiss Ms. Hartshorne from our enquiries. We're aware that your agency has been involved in that case where twelve women were found dead. And now with these latest murders, you understand, it's just formality."

"Wait. How is Sarah linked?" Darren asked sternly.

"CCTV security cameras at two separate locations have her speaking to the victims. The times recorded show clearly that she must have been the last person to see either of them alive, other than the killer. Whatever she may know could prove valuable."

The officer then got up, grabbing a Police radio, and stared at Darren, "It's all at the precinct. Let's take a trip down there, and we can discuss things, in you might say, more appropriate surroundings." – he glanced to Patricia as he spoke.

"Blake?" She retorted.

Darren got up, and walked towards her before brushing past, "I gotta do this. Maybe it'll explain things in my head, all the shit. Contact David. Let him know everything." He said, then proceeded into his bedroom for a change of clothes.

Patricia sighed, and looked to the officers as they waited patiently, the one smiling to her, and she forced a smile in return.

Patricia saw Darren and the two Police Officers out, and Darren smiled back at her.

"Don't worry … I'm sure it's nothing." Patricia said.

Darren nodded, joining the officers, then Patricia watched them leave before closing the door. She turned away and walked over to the phone, then lifted the receiver to her ear.

A station wagon pulled into the long driveway at David's beach house and came to a halt behind two sleek sports cars. At the wheel was a middle-aged housekeeper, a Spanish woman by the name of Estelle. She climbed out taking two bags with her, and stepped onto the tarmac, her shoe crunching fragments of glass.

Estelle then reacted to the sound of a distant telephone ringing and walked obliviously up the drive and slowed down as she saw the broken patio door, and a further carpet of broken glass before her.

"Oh no…" She remarked, and approached, the sound of the telephone growing louder as she reached the framework.

As she stepped inside, she failed to notice the remnants of blood that had not entirely been washed away by the previous night's storm, and as she glanced around on entering the hallway, she backed off to a telephone fixed to the wall next to the kitchen doorway.

Confused and concerned, she turned, then reached up to the phone, but it then rang off before she could answer it.

"Señor David? Are you home?" She called in a thick Spanish accent.

Back at the apartment, a frustrated Patricia hung up the telephone, then noticed Darren's cell on the same small table. She picked it up, flipping the lid and a brief tune announced its operation. She scanned the display, ignoring the bare breasted pin-up chosen for his background, and clicked through some stored numbers, until she found David's. She selected it, then held the phone to her ear, feeling increasingly helpless.

"Where the fuck are you, David?" She whispered as the other end began to ring.

Estelle entered the living area and it was immaculate – not a single thing out of place. She sighed, approached the window, where blinds were drawn, and opened them by pulling a cord at one end. Sunlight drenched the room, and she looked around herself again, until another ringing was heard, this time a standard Nokia ringtone – and it was coming from some distance away.

Hoping it would be David or someone who knew where he might be, she followed the noise out of the room, into the hallway then back out onto the drive. The tune was a little clearer as she walked past the two cars, then proceeded around the side of the house, following a path. She reached two large dustbins, and paused when she realised the tune was coming from inside. At first, she hesitated to grab the lid, but with grim determination, threw the lid back to reveal several large black bin liners that bulged their contents. Flies hit her in the face, causing her to shout out and wave her hands wildly. Then refocusing, her breath was uncontrolled, nerves playing hell. The tune continued, and she stepped forward, grabbing at the bulging bags, before digging her fingernails in, and tore one open to reveal a denim pocket. The cell phone peeked out of it, and with shaking hand, she pulled it free, and went to answer it – but it rang off.

Estelle cursed to herself, and tossed the phone to the floor, breaking it. She then went about tearing at a second bulging bag, until she staggered away with her hand clasped to her mouth, mumbling something in Spanish. A bare foot protruded from the bin

*

At the Police Precinct not a mile from the Detective Agency, Darren was led down a corridor by the two officers and an older, grey-haired Detective by the name of Davenport. They entered a large office and Darren immediately noticed a display on the wall, showing photographs from the scene of each murder, along with various bloody victim shots. He couldn't help but feel repulsed.

"I understand you're a busy man, Mr Thomas." Davenport remarked, a man with a slight hunch to his posture who approached the wall, looking at the photographs.

Darren turned away, "Just get to the point, Detective." He replied.

Davenport looked back at him, then pulled out a chair behind a desk, sitting down.

"This case has really put the cat amongst the pigeons. No real leads and plenty of loose ends. The murders up to now seem entirely random; with the only thing to link them being a weapon and the fact, the hooker and the wine bar owner were related. Brother and sister in-fact."

"So where does my fiancé fit into all of this? Your badges mentioned something about CCTV?"

"We have some photographs taken from CCTV cameras that place your fiancé with two of the victims, only a short while before both ended up dead. What we need to know is, what she was doing there, and whether or not she knew these two people."

Davenport then took a file out of a tray and opened it before him. He passed Darren one photograph, black and white, showing Sarah with Andy at the Gas Station. Darren studied the picture and sighed. As Davenport watched him, for seemingly like an age, he began to notice tears in his eyes.

"Mr Thomas – are you alright?"

Darren sniffed, then lowered the photograph.

"It don't mean nothing. To me it looks like Sarah just got talking to some guy at the Gas Station … doesn't mean a thing."

"Your fiancé was seen at this same location on two occasions; first to leave with this African / American, and secondly to return for her vehicle."

"I… I think she has spoken to the guy once or twice. He runs, I mean 'he ran' that bar by where I work and live." – his thoughts and suspicions were beginning to get to him.

"So, you recognise the man?"

"He and his brother are big players in this town; everyone knows that, and the kinda guys who make enemies. Take your pick from any number of suspects."

Davenport relaxed back in his chair, and then examined the second photograph.

"You became emotional just now. What were your feelings?"

"What do you mean?" Darren retorted defensively, his eyelids a little red.

"Just now…"

"Listen to me." Darren then said, sitting forward, "Sarah and I have been having problems of late. I love her, but she's too involved with her job. I have not spoken with her in two days, and that is not the way it's ever been for us. We're normally inseparable - no matter our work commitments. Works been tougher than this before, but it has never got in the way. I can't explain any of this and to be honest, it's tearing me apart. So yeah, seeing her just now, it affected me. What was you expecting?"

Darren looked like he could break down there and then, but somehow kept himself together. Davenport did understand, as he had had relationship problems himself, but there were still questions that needed answering.

"Alright. Let's try and focus here, Mr Thomas. This photograph is something you need to see also."

He then passed Darren another picture, black and white again, showing Sarah with Lelaina, the hooker, outside the rear entrance to the wine bar. Darren turned it around to look at, and this time he could not give a reasonable impression for what he was seeing.

"What was she doing? Is the hooker a friend?"

"She's hardly got anything on. What is this?" Darren replied, stunned.

"On that night, were you with her at all?"

"She slept over I remember, because I had a nightmare. When I awoke, she wasn't in bed… but she was there. She comforted me."

"She wasn't in bed?"

"Not when I awoke, no – but she wasn't exactly dressed either. Least of all not for taking a walk."

"Was she like she was in the photo?"

"I think so. I can't remember everything clearly. I don't know what any of this is supposed to mean."

"Maybe it doesn't mean anything. We just need to speak to her, Mr Thomas, and clear this matter up once and for all."

Darren just stared at the picture with tearful eyes, trying to see something, to find some hidden truth. He was afraid of what he might discover.

XVIII

At the apartment, Patricia carried some broken ornaments and a burst cushion (feathers still poured out of it) into an open closet opposite Darren's bedroom door, and stuffed them into a bag. She sighed as she stood up straight, wincing slightly as a muscle in her back twinged. Damn, had she got that from being with David? Walking back out, she pushed Darren's door open.

Inside it was dark as the drapes still hung closed from the previous night, and bedclothes were discarded to the floor along with beer cans and women's underwear, hopefully belonging to Sarah. She entered and began to collect various items and place them on the bed, then paused as she saw something peeking out from underneath. She got down on her knees then to her shock, retrieved a rolled up, blood-stained blouse, complete with burnt holes that she wasn't completely sure the identity of. Patricia unravelled the blouse and discovered Sarah's diary within. She sat back on her haunches not knowing what to think. Had something happened to Sarah? Was that why Darren was so terribly upset and self-destructive? It would explain a lot, what with the Police also making an appearance. She prayed he hadn't done something stupid.

Patricia got up, leaving the blouse and diary on the floor. Still feeling tired, thoughts lingering of comforting a helplessly distraught man, an evening she really hoped she'd never have to endure again. She cared for Darren, in a way she wasn't entirely comfortable with, knowing how his past had probably broken him one too many times. She knew how vulnerable he could be, or at least appear to be. It was ground she had trodden before, but this time she could not be sure where it might lead.

Patricia realised to re-awaken her senses at least, she would need a shower. On entering the bathroom, she removed her gown, standing naked before the cubical, and switched on the shower head. At first, it let out a freezing cold spray that made her flinch, but as she let it run over her hand, the water began to warm. She smiled, then stepped under the spray, closing her eyes and letting the water hit her face before turning to drench her long hair in its entirety.

Another set of hands, other than her own, then wrapped around her body and fondled her breasts. With a gasp she opened her eyes and felt breath against her neck. Someone was in the shower with her! She peered back to discover Sarah, her own hair clinging to her face, equally naked as herself.

For some reason, her presence was not the shock it should have been, and her massaging hands just made a pulse tingle in Patricia's belly and caused her nipples to harden.

"What is this?" Patricia asked.

"Relax." Sarah whispered back, then kissed her on the shoulder, and one hand dropped from her breast to touch Patricia between the legs, who jolted in response.

"This isn't happening." She breathed, then felt a finger probe between the lips of her vagina, pressing for entry.

A second finger joined the first. Patricia found herself parting her legs, relaxing against the warmth of Sarah as she felt fingers part her labia, rubbing at her clit which pulsed and engorged under Sarah's manipulation.

"You need to be awoken, Patricia…" Sarah whispered into her ear, "You need release to see more clearly – to see things not yet seen."

The hand was taken from her vagina, and an agonising number of seconds passed by, all the time Patricia just craving its return. Then from behind, between her legs, the hand returned, and this time more fingers - Patricia unsure how many, inserted themselves deep. She opened her legs wider, feeling weakened by the intrusion, but unable, or unwilling, to stop it. Sarah's hand was now inside her, its wrist stretching the mouth of her vagina more than any woman, outside of childbirth, could imagine. Patricia surrendered to the intense feelings – the intense pleasure, as she stood with her legs bent at the knees … and the hand, no, the limb – began to move in and out, giving her the most invasive penetration she'd ever experienced.

Suddenly visions, brought on by the impending promise of orgasm, began to flash in her head, moulding themselves to her own surreal reality. She was walking up a corridor. It looked like a hotel, by its grand décor. On turning a corner, Police tape prevented entry. Patricia looked beyond, and then saw Forensic experts in white overalls. One had a mask over his face, then another exited a room and vomited violently.

Patricia screwed her face up as her body bucked back and forth. *Jeez, how deep was it?* The mouth of her vagina stung as it was stretched to its limit, and her head was racing. Her body began to quiver. Oh, she was incredibly near. She then found herself watching from across a road, seeing two Police cars parked before a house, and a Spanish woman was crying and being comforted by a female Police officer. Then she was looking into David's eyes, as he was fucking her, sweat glistening on his taught, muscular chest.

Patricia staggered in the cubical and had to support herself with both hands to the Perspex walls. It was incredible, the total feeling of fullness … her head felt like it might explode, and her heartbeat hammered her chest.

She saw herself unravelling the map of New York City, yet this time it was transparent, with Darren's desk visible beneath. She walked over to the wall, then placed it directly over a hanging map of Miami. The five points of the star she had previously discovered by joining each murder location with a red line, matched the three locations shown on the other map, and signified two more locations, although the image was blurred and Patricia couldn't be sure. Her face then met the wall of the cubical as her arms gave way. She yelled out then grunted, eyes springing open as orgasm hit her full force.

A rush of feelings flooded her body, an orgasm even stronger than the one with David, and her legs went limp, causing her to slide to the marble floor of the shower. She lay breathless, resting against the wall as warm water rained down from above.

With a slight tremble lingering on her skin, she exhaled slowly.

"Oh God… Sarah, that was…"

She looked up, squinting in the spray, and frowned to discover - she was alone.

*

Shortly afterwards, Patricia, wearing her cream trouser suit, sat at the wheel of Darren's Honda as she pulled out of the driveway to the apartment building. Looking to the city as cars whizzed by, her head was mush, like coming down from a drugs binge. She couldn't decide if what had happened was her fantasising over Sarah, or it had been real; either way the visions she'd experienced were telling her something. A song played on the radio, and she waited for a bus to pass, then drove out onto the road.

As the Honda disappeared into the distance, an engine revved across the road, and a small Jeep pulled away from the kerb, driving into the underground car park.

Eventually the elevator door opened, and a woman disguised in a head scarf and sunglasses, complete with a long raincoat, exited and marched swiftly down the corridor. Reaching the apartment door, the woman raised a gloved hand, inserting a key in the lock and turning it. She entered the hallway, closing the door silently behind her, then walked into the kitchen. She removed her shades, revealing herself as Sarah, and pocketed them inside her coat. Her hair was completely hidden under the scarf.

"Think you're fuckin' clever, huh?" She then said out loud, and bent down to the washing machine, and reached a hand inside.

She felt around for a moment, then cursed, taking out a pair of knickers, and stood up again.

"Bitch!" She said, letting the knickers slip from her hand to land on the tiled floor.

Sarah marched back out and entered the living room. She stopped in mid-stride, looking around, and took a moment to think.

"You really think that's got me? Huh? What were you thinking? By planting that piece of shit evidence, that it could stop us? It could stop me? You have no idea who the fuck you are dealing with, honey." She exclaimed, then walked back out.

Sarah entered the bedroom and approached the bed. Beer bottles still littered the carpet – yet the blouse and diary were gone.

"I needed help, we need help." She then said in a more sorrowful tone, her eyes full of pathetic desperation.

She raised a gloved hand, looking at it, "I don't know what I am anymore. It must stop – I can't go on. Please don't make me." She added.

Her hand then closed into a fist, and her expression changed, "Listen to yourself, you snivelling cunt! You are an embarrassment to us. I can make us strong. I can make us alive! Without me, you're just a needy little bitch chained to a relationship without meaning and a job with no respect. You let your boss fuck you and your fiancé use you to hold on to what little identity he still has left. Haven't you seen the way he looks at that woman? You really think he just wants her as a friend?"

"Fuckin' bitch!!" She then cursed, and grabbed at her own face, causing her to stagger across the room, then threw herself to the floor.

Sarah punched herself in the stomach, grunting with the impact, then rolled over, and slapped herself hard across the face. She snarled, getting up on her knees, then her hand grabbed at her throat, and she began to throttle herself until she was choking.

She tried to crawl over to a small cupboard, then her other hand grabbed the alarm clock off the top, and slammed it against her hand, freeing herself of its grip on her neck. However, the hand retaliated, and punched her square in the face. She fell back against a wardrobe, and the hand grabbed her by the head scarf, and rammed the back of her head until it split the wood of the door.

"Stop it, Sarah!!" She cursed, eyes watering, "You're only hurting yourself!!"

Opening her mouth, she bit herself on the hand as it went to grab at her face again, and she let go, immediately crying out.

"No! You are not in control of me!!" She cursed, blood dripping from one nostril as she slowly got back up, leaning breathlessly against the wardrobe door. She looked around the room. On one side was a table, which she then walked over to, pulling open a drawer.

"What are you doing?" She asked herself, confused.

Her eyes widened, looking exhausted, "I'm ending this." She replied, taking out a paperknife.

"Wait – you're not thinking straight!"

Her hand was shaking as she raised the knife, "No, for once, I actually am thinking straight."

She then turned the blade in on herself and gritted her teeth. Suddenly, her other hand grabbed her wrist, and stopped her just short of plunging the blade into her chest,

"I think you are forgetting something, dear…" She then gasped, her face going red as she struggled and sweat formed on her brow, a strand of blonde hair having fallen free of the scarf.

"What?" She asked.

"Your time here is over." She then said, and the knife dropped from her hand, ricocheting off the table before landing on the floor.

Dropping both arms, Sarah relaxed against the end of the bed. As she caught her breath, slowly, a grin began to form.

"For a minute there," – she swallowed, "You almost had me."

IXX

Patricia arrived in a side street next to the Detective Agency, and switched off the engine. For a moment, she sat at the wheel feeling scared. She did not know what she was doing there, what she thought she might find, but needed to answer the questions plaguing her mind. She climbed out of the car and walked towards a door.

Pausing before it, she raised a set of keys, and unlocked the door. Then as she opened it, an alarm was raised – like she wasn't on edge enough! Patricia reached to a control panel, whilst retrieving Darren's wallet from her jacket pocket, quick to remove a slip of paper with a number written on it. She typed the number on a keypad, and the alarm was silenced. With a sigh, she entered the properly, closing the door behind her.

Within minutes, a sheet of large transparent paper was fed out of a printer on a desk in Darren's office. Patricia grabbed it, then walked over to the wall, and raised it up to place directly over the map of Miami. She held it in place with one hand then applied several drawing pins, until it stayed there by itself. She took a step back.

Patricia examined what was presented to her, eyes jumping from one murder to the other, pinpointed on the map overlaying the other map. A prostitute's murder matched the deaths of the women at the hotel. A musician's murder matched the murder of the prostitute at the wine bar. A student's murder then matched the murder of the hooker's brother at his house. It was a pattern that mirrored events in both cities, with the only thing separating them being six years. Patricia was amazed and more than a little pleased with herself.

She then looked to where two other incidents, forming the two remaining points of the pentagram, landed on the Miami map. One pointed to a street at the edge of the main city … but she wasn't aware of anything happening there, yet maybe it signified future events? It unnerved Patricia what she was discovering. Looking to the final location, she had to move closer to be sure. The point of the pentagram showed a hospital in Brooklyn, however on the Miami map, it seemed to land exactly on a hill over-looking the beach. It was then she realised what was located on that hill - David's beach house.

"No. Oh please God, please no…" She gasped.

A cotton swab was raised to Sarah's bloody nostril, and she winced as it made contact. Replacing the swab on the wash basin in the bathroom, she picked up a hand towel, and ran it under the faucet; blood discolouring the flow of water, then wiped what stains still lingered, until her face could at least appear as it once was. She examined her reflection, some swelling around her left eye remained, but she guessed it would be good enough as long as she avoided close inspection.

In the elevator meanwhile of the apartment building, Darren stood silently pondering his thoughts, none of which he wanted in his head. He knew now he needed to explain things to Patricia. She had already seen and heard enough, seeing how easily broken he could be, how fragile he really was – it was time she knew everything.

Sarah slowly removed her head scarf, allowing the soft silk to drape over the wash basin. The reason for wearing such an item then became clear by the unusual scaly texture having formed on her neck and shoulders, and brilliant-white strands of hair now mixed with her natural blonde. She then reached back and felt her head, before re-examining her hand to discover more blood. Obviously, the impact with the wardrobe door had done more damaged than first anticipated. She had to be careful, she couldn't risk losing this body, at least not while there was still work to be done. Sarah then took a needle and thread from the shelf, and began to apply it to her head, using her other hand to part her hair back. Squirming as the needle pierced flesh, she pushed it in, then drew it back out, running the thread through. Her left eye bulged every time she dug the needle in a little too far, but the pain just willed her on.

Darren reached his apartment door and raised a key. His hand tremored as he went to insert it in the lock. A side-effect of his growing nerves or a developing drink problem? *Both could be right*, he thought. Eventually he pushed the key into the lock and turned it. The front door opened into the hallway, and Darren entered. Sarah froze as she stood in the bathroom, and heard the door shut again. Quickly she grabbed the scarf from the basin, and put it back on, tucking her hair away beneath.

"Patricia? We need to talk." Darren announced, and walked into the living room.

He paused, "Patricia – where are you?" He called, then slowly backed off and turned as he re-entered the hallway.

Suddenly he came face to face with Sarah, and gasped on seeing her. She smiled, wearing her shades again, then lowered them to the end of her nose and said, "Hi."

"Sarah…" was all he could say, she really was the last person he expected.

"What's up? Patricia's out. She was gone when I got here. Where you been? Not just rolling in from the agency, are you now?" Sarah added.

"Er, no. Shit, Sarah. What's going on? Where have you been the last couple of days?"

He watched her push her shades back to her face with a finger.

"Work, honey. The case has been taking up all my spare time. Why, did you miss me, or were you more interested in Patricia?"

"Hey, you know it's not like that. What's got into you? Work never used to come between us in the past. What's changed?"

"I dunno. Maybe I've changed. I've adapted. Moving in another direction. Mr Brunt has high hopes for me, and I think we work well together."

"Excuse me? You're not making any sense. You hate your Boss."

"I never said I hated him."

"Maybe not to me." Darren then said quietly.

"What's that?"

He stared at her, feeling angry and confused.

Sarah returned a sympathetic smile, "Listen, babe… it's just been a difficult time for me that's all. I have some stuff to finish at the office, and then we'll talk – tonight, yeah?"

"The Office?" Darren snapped, "It's Sunday. You've never gone in on a Sunday, Sarah. Be reasonable! Can't you see a problem when it is staring you in the face? We need to deal with this thing. We need to deal with it now!"

Darren waited for some kind of emotional response. After a long silence, he bowed his head with exasperation, walking away into the living room. Sarah just remained in the hallway, and watched him walk over to the drink's cabinet, the door hanging off its hinges, the glass cracked. A picture hung on the wall above, showing the two of them in a loving embrace. Darren focused on it for a second, before taking out a bottle, pouring some Whisky into a shot glass. Sarah stepped forward, lingering in the doorway, one gloved hand on the framework.

"Where you been, then?" She asked.

"I've just come back from the precinct. The Police were here earlier."

Sarah suddenly began to feel uncomfortable.

"They were asking a lot of troubling questions." Darren continued, then raised the glass to his lips, and gulped the Whisky down in one go, "About the case, and also about you." He added with a slight grimace.

He then reached into the cabinet again and retrieved a second shot glass.

"Can I fix you something?" He asked.

No reply came.

He wrinkled his brow, and then turned around. Sarah was gone. The glass slipped from his hand, and Darren watched it land on the carpet and roll under the sofa. Eventually he walked out of the living room towards the open apartment door. Exiting, he rushed towards the elevator, slowing to a halt as he saw the doors close.

"Fuck." He cursed.

Patricia was at the wheel of Darren's car as she drove over a set of crossroads then proceeded up a hill towards David's beach house. She gradually slowed her speed as she drew closer, pulse quickening on seeing two Police squad cars blocking the road off near the house. Her fears were starting to overwhelm her. She parked on the other side of the road, shutting off the engine, then climbed out and looked across to the house. She recalled her vision, and once again laid eyes on the Spanish housekeeper being comforted by a female Police officer. Patricia noticed an ambulance, and her heart went in her mouth.

"No…" She remarked with disbelief, then walked away from the car, until a Police officer approached, and she met with him in the middle of the road, wide Police tape and barricades the only thing separating them.

"Miss? Can we help you? This street is off limits."

"What's happened?" Patricia replied, not looking at him, as she saw the housekeeper get taken to one of the cars and helped inside. She had clearly been crying.

"I'm sorry, I didn't catch your name…" the officer replied.

She focused on his face, "Excuse me? No… I'm a friend… my friend lives here… David Henderson."

The officer frowned, "This road is off limits, Miss. I'm afraid you will have to leave."

Patricia looked to the house again and saw two men in white overalls appear on the patio, removing protective masks from over their nose and mouth. She couldn't stand it any longer, and suddenly ducked under the barriers, and darted away from the officer, despite his yells of protest.

"Miss! Wait! You shouldn't go back there!!"

Patricia then reached the driveway of the house, and met up with the female Police officer, who turned to her in surprise, "Hey, who are you?"

"I knew him! He's my friend!" Patricia exclaimed, and went to rush forward, but the female officer grabbed her.

"No, Miss – stop, you don't want to go in there."

Patricia struggled, then calmed, and they both looked at each other. Tears streamed down Patricia's face.

"Tell me, please. Is he dead?" She begged.

The officer stared at her then sighed, "I'm sorry, Miss. Yes, he's dead."

Patricia cried out, and the officer comforted her, holding her tight, and Patricia sobbed into her chest. After a moment, the officer continued to talk to her.

"Miss. Listen. If you knew him, you'll have to come down to the precinct. Just to fill in the gaps. Will you do that?"

Patricia raised her head. Her face was flushed, and her eyes were wet, "What?"

"This is a murder investigation now. I think you may be able to help."

Patricia just stared at her, unable to think straight. She was devastated.

XX

As it turned late afternoon, Darren walked into his living room, slumping down in his armchair. He raised another Whisky to his lips, and then paused. His memories were catching up with him.

Six years ago, Darren had a nice house in Brooklyn, New York. A failed marriage behind him, he had turned his back on a career in the NYPD as a result. He spent his nights frequenting strip joints or staying at home, getting drunk or jerking off. In many ways, his life should have been over. He had turned to being a Private Detective, having set up business a year previous in the seedy suburb of Springdale, naming the agency 'Blue Circle' as a homage to his favourite TV show, Moonlighting's 'Blue Moon Detective Agency'. Business had not exactly been booming however, be it due to his growing dependency on alcohol or simply a lack of interest. Darren had become self-destructive, and he really only had himself to blame.

One night, just a few weeks shy of his 36th birthday, he was cruising the streets and came upon the figure of an attractive woman, a hooker. He had become accustomed to paying for sex in recent weeks, but for some reason, he pulled over and just observed her, not sexually, but with fascination. She was beautiful, albeit sleazily dressed in leather mini skirt, tight blouse and leather jacket, too much make up, but something about her face, her eyes, and her long black hair presented her in a different light than that of the blonde, disinterested whore he'd met two nights earlier.

As Darren sat sinking further and further into a drunken state, he saw her approach his car, leaning in with what was obviously a rehearsed line of 'You looking for a good time, Mr?'. He welcomed her inside, a slightly older blonde lingering on the sidewalk, a friend most likely, a mentor in the ways of selling oneself for sex.

He could smell her perfume and could feel her presence as he reminisced her sitting in the passenger seat, exchanging pleasantries before he drove away to find a more private rendezvous. That first time, which it turned out was not the last had remained with him for years. If it hadn't been the best sex he'd ever had, it was certainly top three. Maybe also, she was the only woman he had ever truly loved.

Lisa Ann Watts, the hooker was to be labelled a serial killer, and the shock, considering Darren had been investigating the same murders she was committing, whilst simultaneously falling in love with her, destroyed something within that never came back. Those feelings and the regret he felt over that time was still very much a part of him, and the reason he had tried to make a new life and a new name for himself as someone else, this Blake Thomas person. Now though, with recent events and suspicions tapping away at his fragile psyche, the real Darren Maitland was starting to come back, and he realised it was just a matter of time before his mask of sanity would start to slip.

6:00pm

Sarah entered the lobby of the Ambassador Hotel, dressed in the same long raincoat and with the scarf still concealing most of her identity, along with the shades. She smiled to a woman at the check-in desk, and took out a purse, quick to reveal a gold credit card.

"I assume you take all major plastic?" She announced, and the woman nodded.

"Yes Ma'am, how can I be of service today?"

"A reservation, under the name 'Smith'."

The woman checked her computer, "Ahh yes, the penthouse suite. Just the one night, Miss?"

"Yes."

The woman tapped away on the keyboard, then Sarah handed her the card.

At the Police precinct meanwhile, a door opened, and the female officer peered in. Patricia had been allowed to sleep after the devastating news of David's murder, and she squinted her eyes as the outer light hit her in the face.

"Ms. Willis?" the Officer asked, "Detective Davenport is ready to see you now."

Patricia sat up on the surprisingly comfortable sofa she had been offered. Her eyes were still sticky from the tears she had shed.

Soon Patricia, her cream suit looking dishevelled and creased, sat before a desk in an office, as Detective Davenport stood by the window. The sun light was fading. It would be dark soon, he realised. He raised a plastic cup of coffee to his lips - then Patricia cleared her throat.

"Have you any idea who the killer is yet?" She asked, the words tumbling from her mouth still not sounding believable to her.

Davenport turned, "I have some theories." He replied.

"You know I can't help you. I've pieced a few things together, but I still don't know where to point the finger."

"Detective work, Miss Willis," Davenport announced, and pulled out a chair, sitting down, "is like being presented with a thousand-piece jigsaw puzzle. At first, it can be intimidating, impossible. But the more pieces you put together, sooner or later a picture is formed."

Patricia was beyond stupid speeches. She felt bitter, angry – just wanting to hit out at something, or someone, and the way this guy was going, he would be an easy target.

"Listen. Something big is going to happen." She then said sternly, sitting forward, "The murders mirror five murders that took place in New York six years ago. Something bad was going down at that time, it was leading to something. I guess whatever the plan was, it never came to fruition, so now we come to today."

"What are you talking about?" Davenport enquired.

"The cult deaths were not just coincidence, Detective. They brought something or 'someone' back, to complete work that begun all those years ago. If the circle is allowed to complete, God knows what will happen."

"Wait a minute. Are you serious? What happened six years ago?"

"Have you ever heard of a woman called Lisa Ann Watts?"

"No. Should I have?"

"Yes, Detective. She was a prostitute who murdered some people, but was later killed after trying to flee a hospital. Most of what went down has either been covered up or forgotten about, but she had tapped into something. Something unholy."

"Now hang on a minute. Are you on drugs?"

Patricia sighed with exasperation, then got up, turning away to the door for a moment to gather her bearings. She then looked back.

"There is a pattern, Detective, and a higher purpose to all of this. We must find out who the killer is and stop whatever the fuck is about to take place."

Davenport looked stunned, then after a brief pause, he got up, "I think I have some material you should see, Ms. Willis." He replied, then walked out of the room.

Back at the Hotel, Sarah came out of a room within the luxury penthouse suite, to the sound of the door knocking. She had changed into a black robe with the hotel name embroidered in gold on the breast pocket, and her hair was concealed under a short black wig. She then opened the door and was presented with the sight of Montgomery Brunt, wearing a perfectly tailored, grey suit and a big smile. Oh how he disgusted her, but she faked enthusiasm.

"Mr Brunt! I've been waiting for you." She said.

Montgomery stepped forward, "Sarah! Like the wig, are we going to play a game?" He remarked, and raised his hand, curling it around the back of her neck, and leaned in for a kiss.

She then jolted, stepping back. He wrinkled his nose with confusion.

"What is it?" He asked, not aware of the scales that had formed beneath her hair and continued under the silk of her collar.

"Nothing. Let's not rush things. We have all evening. Why don't you go into the bedroom?" She asked.

"I'm sorry. I understand. I'll be gentle." He replied creepily, then glanced down to her right hand, noticing it was wrapped in bandage.

"What have you done to your hand?" He asked.

Sarah raised it, and cradled it defensively against herself, then an image flashed in her head of her sinking her teeth into her own leather-clad hand.

"Just a burn from my iron at home. Nothing serious." She lied.

Montgomery smiled, then walked past her, and entered a grand bedroom, with a large four-poster bed in the centre, tropical fish in a lit-up tank by the wall, and gentle violin music playing from a sound system somewhere.

"Perfect." He remarked quietly to himself, whilst subconsciously messing with his wedding ring on his finger.

Patricia entered another office, the same office Darren was led into, with photographs creating a macabre mural on the facing wall. Patricia stared at the pictures, but was not shocked. The past few days seemed to have desensitised her to such imagery.

"What is it, Detective?"

"A suspect. We spoke to your friend, Mr Thomas earlier, but he had little to add. I guess the shock and confusion was too much for him."

He handed Patricia a file, and she took it, turned it around, then opened it as she stood beside the desk. She cast her eyes on the CCTV photos of Sarah. *It all seems to make sense now*, she thought.

"It's her." She said.

"What do you mean?"

"I don't know why, but something or someone has been pointing me in this direction, and there's a strong feeling I have, that I am looking at David's killer."

"You realise it sounds ridiculous to even think of this woman as being capable of these murders."

"She is seen here with two of the victims, and she also knew David through Blake. She is the only possibility. It would also explain why Blake has been having trouble and isn't exactly stable right now."

Davenport stared at her, and couldn't help but admire her drive. Then after a moment, he lifted a telephone receiver from the table, and tapped in a number on the keypad.

"Johnson, its Davenport. Any news from the stake out at the Hartshorne house?" He asked.

"Nothing yet, Sir. Nobody has been in or out, if they had, you would have known by now."

"We need to take this lady in for questioning immediately. Keep me posted."

Patricia closed the file in her hands and looked at the Detective again, "She's my friend's fiancée. I know how bad it sounds for me to accuse her like this, but nothing else seems to fit the way this does. Maybe if we spoke to her, something would slip."

Davenport nodded, realising this woman might be onto something.

XXI

Montgomery Brunt was excited and nervous all at once, lying spread eagled on the large double bed, having been stripped to his boxer shorts, a blindfold over his eyes, and all four limbs tied with fur-covered cuffs to each post. His large body was in good shape for a man of his age; his chest gently sprinkled with subtle grey hairs, his skin bronzed and leathery from too many sun-drenched vacations.

He could hear classical music playing in the background, and his senses were heightened as he lay in anticipation.

He heard a door open, as Sarah walked into the dimly lit room, still wearing the gown and the black wig over her hair, now complete with dark make up about her eyes and dark red lipstick.

"Mr Brunt. Are you relaxed?" She asked.

Montgomery chuckled playfully, "Oh yes. What are you going to do?"

Sarah smirked, "Oh, where to begin." She replied, stepping before the end of the bed, and slowly undid the rope belt at her waist. Her gown dropped to her ankles, revealing her firm, toned body in nothing more than an embroidered thong accentuating her perfect round ass. However, as the curve of her back arched up to her shoulder blades, a grizzlier sight was beheld. Two old bullet wounds lay decaying, the skin splintered and cracking like the fragile surface of crème brulei. A patchwork of reptilian-like scales had also formed around her neck and shoulders.

She inhaled deeply, her spine and ribs bulging through thinning flesh as if ready to burst. She then breathed out and climbed forward onto the bed.

Montgomery groaned, his wildest fantasies attempting to predict what was about to happen, but blissfully ignorant of Sarah's true intentions. She crawled over the full length of his body, and brought her face down to his chest. A long, serpent-like tongue came out to lick a trace of sweat.

"So, Mr Brunt, how long have you fantasised about a night such as this?"

"Ever since I met you, your first day in the office. You were so innocent and juvenile."

He understood the game, he had played it many times before.

"Is that so?"

"Yes."

"I have sucked on your cock. Is that where I should start?"

"Be my guest."

"Maybe I should nibble your earlobe." Sarah continued.

"Yes. I'd like that."

"You look good enough to eat." She added.

Montgomery sniggered, "Oh yeah? Feel free – all you can eat buffet."

Sarah grinned and sat up. She then removed her wig, and her once blonde hair fell free, now a brilliant white. It was a striking image. She stared down at her prey, not blinking, totally focused.

"Tell me, Mr Brunt..." She said, then reached forward, snatching the blindfold from his eyes, and he gasped, laying eyes on her afresh.

He was shocked by her hair, and then looked down, taking in the sight of her pert breasts, the nipples erect. Suddenly he clasped eyes on the vile decay of a further bullet wound in her stomach; her navel was gone, and red veins bulged through the skin, the opening leaking puss, and the smell began to drift under his nostrils. He convulsed, then looked back up to see that Sarah's pupils were glowing.

"Do you think me sexy now?" She asked, and opened her mouth to reveal a mass of jagged, razor-sharp teeth.

"Jesus Christ!" Montgomery remarked, and Sarah swooped down on him, sinking the full force of her powerful jaws into his neck – a spray of blood shooting into the air like a fountain.

Meanwhile, Patricia sat at the wheel of Darren's car and arrived outside Sarah's house. It had begun to get dark, and as she switched off the headlights, two Police squad cars turned up in front of her. She sighed, unfastening her seat belt, then climbed out. She met up with Detective Davenport on the sidewalk before of a row of white picket fencing. No lights were visible in the windows, and only the hum of car engines could be heard, along with a distant hoot of an owl.

"She's not been in or out all the time we've watched the place. Her neighbours have seen neither hide nor hair. What we doing here, Ms. Willis?" Davenport asked.

"There could be some clue, a scrap of information. Whatever she's been planning up to now – and there is a plan, Detective, I'm sure of that. Therefore, the answer could be lying inside."

"Ok. I'll get my boys here to break the door in."

Patricia held up a set of car keys.

"Relax. Let me try one of these first." She said, then proceeded up the driveway.

Soon the door opened in the hallway, and Patricia peered hesitantly inside. She listened carefully. A sound of a clock ticking reached her ears, but nothing else. She opened the door further, then stepped inside, followed closely by Davenport. He revealed a revolver.

"What's that for?"

"You can't be too careful." He replied.

Patricia walked towards the kitchen door, and tried the handle. The door opened easily, and she looked in. The work surfaces were untouched, and immaculately clean. However, for some reason, she failed to notice a short, small figure of a child, standing in the centre of the darkened room, wide eyes transfixed. It was the girl who had died, Jessica. As Patricia eased the door shut, the girl reacted, reaching out with one hand and stepping forward. As the door closed, her fingers touched the wood, and she whispered "Mommy?"

At Darren's apartment, he came out of the bedroom wearing an overcoat, then approached the door, and jolted as an intercom buzzed. He sighed, pressing the button.

"I'm coming. Give me a break, will ya?"

"No problem, Sir, but the metre is running." a voice replied in a Mexican accent.

He glanced back down the hall to where light emitted from the living room. He almost felt like the place was not his anymore – nothing was the same without Sarah. He opened the door, pausing before he left.

"This ends tonight..." He remarked, then stepped out, closing the door behind him.

Eventually Darren exited the building by the front door, and descended the steps, walking towards a cab where a plump Mexican driver stood smoking a fat cigar.

"You ready, Mr? Where we heading?" the driver asked, his words mixing with thick clouds of smoke.

"I'll explain on the way." Darren replied, not even looking at the man, and walked around to the passenger side, opened the door and climbed in.

Back at the house, Patricia left the bedroom just as Davenport descended the stairs.

"Anything?" She asked.

"The closets have been cleaned out. Wherever she was going, she wasn't planning on comin' back any time soon."

Patricia then walked past the phone, and a gust of wind from the open front door blew a piece of note paper off a small table, and she immediately looked at it as it drifted to the floor.

"What is it?" Davenport asked.

Patricia knelt down, then picked the paper up, turning it over, and read what was written.

"I don't know. There's a time here, and a name of a hotel."

"What Hotel? Let me see that." Davenport said and rushed forward.

Patricia stood up and handed him the note.

"The Ambassador. That's not far from here." He gasped.

Darren looked stern and focused as he sat alongside the driver, music on the radio of a station only Mexicans probably listened to. The driver offered him glances that were never returned, and had the good sense to not ask questions.

"Take a left up here." Darren then ordered.

The driver nodded, and changed gear before doing what he was told, and paused at a set of traffic lights. A pair of dice hung from the mirror, fashionable long before the driver had got the job, and out of fashion ever since.

"It's a nice night. Plenty of pussy walks these streets. I know some people if you want fixing up…"

Darren slowly looked over to him, then the lights changed again, and the cab proceeded on its way. They continued down a darkened road that led out of the city. Darren looked around cautiously, and then reached a hand inside his jacket.

"Stop the cab." He said.

"Excuse me?"

"Stop the cab."

"Here? But this ain't nowhere." the driver added.

"I know – now stop the cab!"

The cab then screeched to a halt, and the driver looked nervously at his passenger, who was pointing a gun clearly big enough to take his head off.

"Wait. Mr. What is this?" He gasped.

"Relax. I'm taking this vehicle. Get out now, and you can still go home and fuck your wife. Give me any shit, and you won't have a dick to fuck her with."

The door opened on the road, and the driver climbed out hastily. He mumbled in Mexican whilst backing away.

"Thanks." Darren then said, reaching over and pulling the door shut, moving into the driver's seat, then trod down on the accelerator.

A cloud of dust and gravel announced his departure.

XXII

Shortly afterwards, Patricia was following Davenport's car, sandwiched between it and two other squad cars. She had thought a lot about what she was doing, what it could mean and how it might affect Darren. She felt bad, but despite her reluctance around making it personal - after David, Sarah had to be stopped. She clutched Darren's cell phone in her hand and selected the number of his apartment from the display, then raised the phone to her ear. After a brief pause, the other end began to ring. She looked to the car directly in front, then heard Darren's voice.

"Darren… it's Patricia, are you…"

She then realised something as his voice continued. It was his answer phone message.

"Fuck." She cursed, waiting for her turn to talk, then added: "If you're there Darren? Fuckin' pick up!"

She waited, lacking patience, before lowering the phone and ending the call.

On a stretch of road, Darren drove watching the houses, staring accusingly at passers-by. In his paranoid state of mind, they were all Sarah, mocking him, playing some kind of game. He didn't know what he was doing either. Did he believe the thoughts in his head? Or did he actually just want to hold her again, and tell her everything was going to be alright? He adjusted the gears, then trod down on the accelerator, speeding onwards.

The Ambassador Hotel

7:55pm

Patricia climbed out of Darren's car to be met by Detective Davenport, who was stood looking up to the sky. She frowned at him as she closed the driver's side.

"What time do you make it?" He asked.

"A little before eight – why?"

"It's the middle of summer, but look at this shit…"

Patricia glanced up to the sky, and to her disbelief, she saw dark, rolling clouds forming, blocking out what little sunlight remained, slowly sinking all around into night.

"Damn…" She remarked.

"I've got a bad feeling." Davenport added and looked at Patricia.

"Let's get inside. Maybe a storm's brewing." She said.

Soon they walked through the grand open-plan lobby of the hotel, and approached a booking-in desk, where the same woman who had checked Sarah in, stood chatting to a bellhop.

"Excuse me…" Davenport then interrupted, grabbing the woman's attention.

"Yes Sir, how may I help you?" She replied with a well-rehearsed smile.

"We believe a lady may be staying here, blonde hair, in her late twenties to early thirties."

"Oh I see, and you are?" the woman retorted.

"Oh, forgive me." Davenport replied, reaching inside his jacket, then revealed his badge, "Detective James Davenport – Miami P.D."

The woman suddenly looked concerned.

"Her name is Sarah Hartshorne, but I'd hazard a guess she'd be staying under a pseudonym."

The woman then opened a register and looked down the list of names. Patricia watched in anticipation. After a moment, the woman shook her head.

"I'm sorry, Detective – there's no Hartshorne staying with us. How did she look again?"

"Blonde hair."

The woman thought for a moment, then looked at the register again, "There was a woman, about thirty, maybe younger who came in, she looked like she was in disguise – was wearing a head scarf and sunglasses. I thought it strange at the time, but…"

"What room?" Patricia then exclaimed.

Davenport looked at her, "You reckon that's her?"

"It's on the sixth floor, room 266 - booked in about two hours ago…"

Patricia then hurried away, and Davenport looked over to three officers who were waiting in the background. He signalled to them, one went back outside, and the other two joined Davenport.

"But, wait…" the woman then called, but was unable to stop them, "She's got a guest." She added, to no avail.

As Darren continued on his journey, he tuned the radio, searching for some normality to take his mind off things. A gentle voice then came on, telling a hard luck story of some woman widowed and left with two children to bring up. Then as he looked ahead again, he gasped on seeing a figure stumble into the road, and he swerved his car, the tires screeching, and he slammed the breaks. Darren's stolen cab skidded to a halt several metres down the street, and he sat panting, not sure if he hit the person or not. After a moment, he unclipped his seat belt, then looked to the rear-view mirror. To his considerable stress, that same figure was walking aimlessly in the middle of the road. Quickly he opened the door and got out, then turned and walked away from the car. As he gradually gained on the figure – he then froze.

It looked like a woman, going by the long flowing, white hair, and she was wearing some sort of black gown, although her feet were bare.

"Hey!" He called.

The woman stopped dead, "You crazy or something? I could have killed you!" He added.

Stepping forward two paces, he then watched as the woman slowly turned around, and just then … all of Darren's hopes and dreams were shattered by the reality of what stood before him. Heavily soaked in more blood than he had ever seen, her gown open to reveal she was naked underneath, was Sarah, her pitiful eyes just returning a look of total bewilderment.

"Sarah…" Darren said after a long silence.

He hurried forward, and she collapsed into his arms, staining him heavily in blood.

"Oh God, what is this – are you hurt?" He cried, cradling her head close to his face, causing more blood to stain his cheek.

"Take me home." She breathed.

Darren soon helped Sarah into the passenger seat, and she held the gown tight as if suddenly aware of herself. He stared at her, unable to fathom the situation unfolding, and closed the door, before walking around to the other side. He climbed in and sat with the engine running. He could hear her breathing. A deep feeling of deja vu then washed over him as something flashed in his head. He saw the black-haired girl, Lisa Watts sitting next to him, equally as bloody and wordless. He closed his eyes for a moment, not wanting to think.

"Blake…" then came Sarah's voice.

He opened his eyes, not looking at her.

"Why aren't we moving?" She asked.

Darren sighed as he reached to pull his seat belt from over his shoulder. Suddenly, he slammed his elbow violently into Sarah's face. The back of her head smacked against the headrest. He hit her two more times, and she slumped to one side – unconscious. Crying out with despair, Darren turned to her and brought a hand up, grabbing her by the jaw. He stared at her with hatred as she lay with her eyes closed, lifeless, but not dead – he knew what he was doing.

"You think you can fuckin' fool me? You think I am fuckin' stupid? This ends tonight!" He shouted.

Back at the Hotel, Detective Davenport led two officers and Patricia Willis down a corridor on the sixth floor, and soon reached the end, until Patricia stopped. Davenport looked back to her – she had gone rather pale.

"What is it?"

"I dunno. I… I feel like I have been here already."

"Excuse me?"

"I know, it sounds stupid, but this corridor, this hotel – I've seen it before."

"You stayed here?"

"No."

Davenport was confused.

"Something bad has happened." Patricia added.

Davenport recognised the seriousness in her face, and the fear, he had seen it many times before. He unsheathed his pistol.

Soon they reached a door, and Patricia backed off to the wall.

Davenport looked at her again, "Relax." He added, then raised a clenched fist, giving the hard wood a knock.

Inside, the narrow hallway was free of sound and movement. The knock came a second time, followed by a much longer pause.

"Miss Smith?" came Davenport's voice.

Nothing.

Suddenly, the door burst open, hitting the wall and swinging back, until the two officers walked in, pistols out, with Davenport and Patricia following cautiously behind.

"Keep your wits about you, guys. If this is what we think it is, we could be dealing with a serial killer, one who most likely will not come quietly."

One officer then entered the bedroom as the other walked forward into the kitchen. A yelp of terror was heard, and Davenport rushed into the bedroom, quickly followed by a very nervous Patricia.

"What is it, Johnson?" Davenport called, then froze in mid-stride as he looked to the bed.

Patricia fell against the wall in total revulsion, as lying on the bed, was what could only be referred to as a carcass – the bloody and half eaten remains of Montgomery Brunt. A faint steam seemed to rise into the air from an exposed rib cage.

Davenport covered his nose and mouth from the smell, and Patricia forced herself to look away.

"What the hell are we dealing with here, sir?" the officer asked.

The other officer then walked in, puzzled, and saw the remains. Quickly he convulsed, covering his mouth, and darted back out, to more than likely empty the contents of his stomach in the outer corridor.

XXIII

It had turned night much sooner than it was expected for the middle of summer. It was an omen, and all around felt it. Darren turned to an unconscious Sarah, slumped with her head to the passenger door window, face as bloody as the rest of her, nose more than likely broken, her bottom lip split. As she lay there, an unmistakable smell exuded from her, like raw meat.

"I was living in a dream." He whispered, touching her cheek tenderly, "Thinking all my demons were gone. To think I could re-invent myself, and turn my back on who, or what, I really am. I understand now, Sarah – you came into my life for a reason. I should have realised it sooner. Things could not carry on much longer the way they had been. It had to stop. I had to wake up."

A tear rolled down his cheek as he realised his whole world, his fake world had revealed its artificiality, like he'd just woke up from The Matrix. He smiled distantly, thinking to better times … for a second he saw his ex-wife's face, 'Eleanor' had been her name. Sitting upright in his seat, he glanced to the mirror, seeing that guy looking back… Blake Thomas. Did he even recognise him anymore?

He had parked the cab in the large forecourt of Miami Police Department. The driver's side opened, and Darren climbed out. He looked up to the sky at the darkness above. Not giving it a second thought, he peered up the towering height of Miami P.D. building, a gentle wind making his coat billow out around him. He then took out his revolver and aimed it back into the cab. He paused, focused on the building, waiting.

After a few seconds, a Police squad car entered, and the headlights lit him up as the officer at the wheel applied the brakes.

"Holey fuck!" The officer exclaimed on seeing Darren.

The car screeched to a halt, and the officer exited, readying his pistol.

"Hey – what's the problem, man?" He called, noticing the blood stains on Darren's shirt.

Darren eased the hammer back on the gun, then held his finger steady on the trigger. If Sarah moved or made the slightest sound, he promised himself she would be dead.

"I have her, Officer, the one you are all looking for!" He called back.

The officer glanced for a second to the building, then saw the entrance doors open, and two more armed officers came out, with one readying a shot gun.

"Drop the weapon, buddy – let's talk." the officer replied, re-focusing on Darren.

"She's a killer. You have to arrest her. She's capable of anything."

"What's this about, man?" the officer added.

"The murders, the killings that have been going down. I have her, the one responsible ... right here."

The officer looked concerned, then backed off. As the two other officers approached, he raised a hand to stop them in their tracks.

"Step away from the cab, sir – we'll take it from here."

"You gotta lock her up – she's crazy – you gotta lock her away."

"We'll handle it, step away from the vehicle and toss the weapon."

Darren then glanced in at Sarah, and she groaned. Suddenly his gun fired, blasting her in the ribs, and she went rigid, rising off the seat with a yelp of pain, then collapsed again.

"Fuck!" the officer cursed, then aimed his gun.

Darren looked back, then gasped as the window to the open door shattered, and he turned and ran behind the vehicle. The gun had fallen from his hand in the process, and he was left crouched behind the cab, panting for breath.

"Ok, drop this fool!" the officer announced, and the two other officers rushed forward, aiming their guns. As Darren poked his head out, a loud blast from the shotgun was heard, which blew a hole in the windscreen and shattered the back window, forcing Darren to the ground.

For a moment all was silent. A crunch of gravel then announced the officers approaching. At the front of the cab, the officer with the shot gun just stared, the cracked glass of the windscreen concealing the interior. The other two then walked around to the passenger side. The first who had arrived by squad car then tried the handle. Suddenly, the door was blown off in its entirety, and the impact smacked the officer's body against a low wall. Then as the door fell to the ground, the other officer, sporting a pistol slowly approached, until a bare foot trod gravel and fragments of glass as Sarah then climbed out, her gown open, her body naked and coated in patches of dry blood. The officer stared with absolute astonishment.

"Who the fuck is that?" the officer with the shot gun then remarked.

"Shoot her!" the other officer shouted, and the shotgun went off, but Sarah just leaped up onto the cab roof, her gown flowing around her like a cape, then she squatted down, hissing like an animal, before leaping forward, landing powerfully on the officer as the shotgun fired again into the air, and he hit the ground hard.

At the back of the cab, Darren slowly got to his feet, and gradually peered over the trunk of the cab, able to see movement through the two shattered windows. As silence was restored, he stood upright, and stepped to one side to see the unconscious officer on the ground with the cab door by his legs. Suddenly, another officer stumbled forward, a hand to his throat as blood flowed all over his uniform. He stared wide eyed to Darren, then collapsed. Darren quickly rushed forward to the front of the cab, and saw the dead third officer, his throat brutally torn out, exposing strands of flesh and bone. He looked ahead to the building, seeing the figure of Sarah sprinting towards the open entrance doors.

"Oh God." He whispered, before grabbing the shot gun out of the officer's limp hands, and hurried after her.

A man in a suit walked down a corridor at the hotel, and was stopped by Police tape that closed off the entrance to the next corridor. Two officers stood guard, as Davenport walked out of the room whilst Patricia was resting against a small chest of drawers by the adjacent wall. She looked traumatised.

"Detective – may I speak with you?" the man asked in a well-spoken, French accent.

Davenport walked over, ducked under the tape and met with him.

"Are you the manager?" He asked.

"That is correct. What is the meaning of this? Has something occurred?"

"I'm afraid this corridor is closed for the foreseeable future – I should even recommend closing the hotel."

"That is impossible – we have nearly 500 guests here at the moment, and at this time of the year, that number could well double in the coming weeks."

"Well, one of your guests here, has been murdered, sir."

The manager looked shocked. A Police radio then crackled, and Patricia looked over to one of the Police officers. He took a radio off his belt and answered it.

"Holmes … what's the problem?"

"Holmes! Is Davenport there? We, er, we got a situation."

"What situation?" the officer asked, visibly still on edge.

The officer's voice on the other end trailed off, and Holmes looked puzzled.

"No! Get away from me …no!!" the voice was heard saying, followed by a terrible scream, a crash and a high-pitched squeal – then silence.

"Fuck. What was that?" Holmes gasped.

Patricia stood up and looked past him to Davenport who's attention had been alerted.

"Holmes – what was that all about?" He asked sternly as the manager remained looking concerned.

Holmes stood messing with his radio, changing frequencies, then sound came back on, wild manic screaming, a further series of crashes, as well as gunshots, followed by a loud blast. Holmes looked back to Davenport as Patricia approached, then after a brief silence, a voice came on.

"Hello? Can anyone hear me? If anyone is there, we need help - repeat, we need help – this is Blake Thomas – over."

Patricia gasped, then snatched the radio out of Holmes' hand, "Blake!!" She exclaimed, pressing a button, and Davenport ducked back under the Police tape to reach her.

"Give me that." He said, just as a voice replied.

"Patricia? Holy hell… Is that you?"

"Blake … where are you?" She asked in desperation.

Davenport looked astonished.

"I'm at the Police precinct. You gotta get help, it's Sarah – she's killing everybody!"

Eventually Davenport, Patricia and Officer Holmes came hurrying out of the entrance doors of the building and quickly made for their vehicles.

"Maybe you should go home, Ms. Willis, this is too dangerous now." Davenport announced.

Patricia stopped by Darren's car and glanced over to Davenport, "What? Like that situation back there was any less dangerous? I'm coming with you whether you like it or not. Blake is there, he'll need my help."

Davenport sighed, climbing into his car as Holmes climbed into the passenger seat.

XXIV

The Police radio crackled in Darren Maitland's hand as he leant against the wall beside the open door of an office he had found shelter in. A pump-action shot gun was held limply in his other hand, every fibre of his being intensified.

"Blake … come in…" a female voice then said, coming from the radio.

Darren exhaled, edging towards the doorway, and peered cautiously into an outer corridor. A faint sound of screaming could be heard, followed by distant gunshots. Looking to the corridor wall, he noticed a thick crimson streak, and a dead officer lay on the tiled floor in a pool of his own blood.

"Speak…" He then slurred, holding the radio to his ear.

"Blake? You alright? Speak to me."

"I'm still alive, if that's what you mean. God, Patricia – it's really fuckin' bad here. Where are you guys?"

"We're on our way. Blake, there's something you need to know."

Darren cradled the shotgun in his arms and held the radio between shoulder and jaw as he slotted in shells, one after the other.

"What?"

"It's David."

"God, where is that asshole? Has he been in contact at all?"

"He's dead, Blake. It was… it was Sarah. I'm so sorry."

Darren paused for a moment, before finishing loading up the shotgun.

"I see."

"We're about two minutes away. I have Detective Davenport with me, and he's called for back up from the other precincts. Just stay alive now – you hear me?"

Darren didn't reply, lowering the radio and switched it off, stepping into the corridor. He proceeded past the dead officer, chambering his shotgun as he walked. Then unbeknownst to him, the dead officer's body began to move, and the eyes sprang open, the pupils clouded over and blood shot. A single vain pulsed in his forehead.

Suddenly, he got up and staggered after Darren, who turned, crying out with horror and fired. The officer was blasted off his feet and hit the floor hard, his stomach having been blown to bits.

"Oh fuck me." Darren remarked, "That didn't just happen."

Outside in the courtyard, two squad cars followed closely by Darren's Honda with Patricia at the wheel, screeched to a halt. Doors opened and weapons were loaded up and chambered. Then an armoured Police van arrived in the outer street, and the back opened, a team of SWAT pouring out, wearing padded jackets, balaclavas and sporting sub machine guns.

"Alright." Davenport announced, "I want this to be quick and to the letter. Fish the suspect out by any means necessary. Preferably I want her alive, but if you have to, lethal force is permitted. But I repeat 'only if you have to."

Patricia emerged from Darren's car and looked over to the cab, noticing the smashed windscreen.

"What about that?" She asked Davenport.

"What about it? It's a cab."

"Maybe there's still someone inside."

"That's the least of my problems, some Mexican prick waiting for his fair."

Patricia sighed. Davenport then walked forward and was handed a rifle. Looking up to the tall building, it at first appeared peaceful and without sound. Suddenly, an office window on the third floor shattered and a female officer was thrown out to plummet and hit the ground metres from where they stood.

"Holy fuck!" He yelled.

Officers rushed over, and one knelt at the Black woman's side. Deep, claw-like scratches disfigured her face. A loud snarl was then heard, and Davenport turned just in time to see one of his men get jumped by another officer, resurrected and now expressing demonic ferocity. An officer who rushed forward was smacked across the face and sent hurtling into the air, then Davenport aimed his rifle, and shouted.

"Hey, you fat fuck!"

The demon officer looked up short of tearing out the other officer's voice box, and received a shot to the forehead, which dropped both of them instantly. Davenport gasped as calm was restored, and then looked around for Patricia.

"Ms. Willis?" He called, and walked back to Darren's car to find Patricia crouched and quivering behind.

"Hey ... are you OK?" He asked, offering a hand.

Tearful, Patricia had plainly seen too much to maintain her emotions any longer. She took Davenport's hand, and was walked out from behind the car.

"Just stick with me, kid, you'll be alright." He reassured, but Patricia wasn't convinced.

Up in the sky above, a helicopter passed over the building. On the roof, more demonic officers shuffled like zombies aimlessly seeking their prey. Ropes dropped and a further SWAT team descended down, opening fire and the demon officers were blasted off their feet with deep, lingering groans from their mouths.

In one corridor, Darren came out of a room, walked forward and entered another, then shot a demon secretary as she got up from behind a desk, where an overweight detective lay with his shirt torn open and his stomach split, entrails spilling onto the floor around him.

"Sarah?" Darren exclaimed, "If you can hear me, I'm coming for you, sweetheart." – then he walked forward through another door into the next corridor, pausing only to check around him, "Yeah, I'm coming for you." He added quietly, walking on.

Davenport entered the reception with Patricia, and the SWAT team hurried forward, kicking a door open, then opening fire on whoever lurked inside.

"Clear." the leader announced.

"What is happening here, Patricia?" Davenport asked.

Patricia stepped forward, and picked up a revolver where a dead clerk was slumped over the counter.

"Hell is happening, Detective." She replied coldly, popping the barrel out to check the load, then popped it back in again with a quick flick of her wrist.

Her radio crackled on her hip. Unhooking it from her belt, she raised it up to speak into.

"Blake?"

"Who's this – this is team Bravo to team Alfa … are you reading me?" returned a voice.

The SWAT team leader then reacted and snatched the radio off Patricia.

"This is Alfa team leader – what is your sit-rep?" He replied.

Patricia just stared at him with anticipation.

"We got a problem. I think we've found the suspect."

In another corridor on a higher floor, a small SWAT team of four had lined up with their backs to the wall, the leader peering into the next corridor.

"Either that or the Miami P.D. has just started recruiting naked witches with killer asses."

"What's she doing?" The other SWAT leader's voice replied.

Bravo team leader looked down the corridor at the sight of Sarah, naked and partially slick with blood, devouring a corpse of a young female secretary, eating her insides like they were succulent cooked meat.

"I'd like to say she's just relaxing, whistling a tune and minding her own business – but she's not. I think the poor girl she's currently eating is only partially dead, going by how her left leg is kicking and shaking."

One of the other SWAT cops then remarked, "Could be an involuntary nerve still reacting. She's gotta be dead, Sir."

Bravo team leader glanced back to him, taking his eyes off Sarah, just long enough for the young secretary to wake up and puke blood. Sarah then jolted, and looked back with a blood-soaked face, a yellow glow emitting from her eyes.

She noticed the shadow of the SWAT team coming from the other corridor, and turned around, squatting on all fours, then moved a little forward, raising herself up on her feet as if ready to pounce.

Bravo team leader looked back at her, gasping at the sudden change of position.

"Fuck. She knows we're here." He said, and backed off.

One SWAT cop sporting a machine gun then stepped out into full view. Only around twenty metres separated him from Sarah and the now sitting upright, half eaten secretary.

"Mother of God." He gasped, then as Sarah waited, poised to attack, the ankles and heels of both her feet crumbled gruesomely, the skin falling away to reveal hooves underneath. Now her transformation was complete.

"What just happened?" the cop remarked, and Bravo team leader came out behind him.

All of a sudden, Sarah galloped forward on all fours, darted up the wall, then launched herself at the officers with a high-pitched shriek. Bravo team leader fired a large pump action shotgun, and it blasted Sarah in the chest, throwing her violently against the wall, before dropping her to the floor.

After a moment, a cloud of smoke cleared, and Bravo team leader stepped forward, reaching for his radio again, and held it to his mouth as he pointed the weapon to where Sarah lay, blood coating the floor and adjacent wall.

"We got her, Alfa team. What's the situation where you are?"

Davenport was following Alfa team leader as they made their way through a large office with various cubicles.

"They suddenly just stopped. I take it you've seen the zombies."

"Our hit ratio has clocked in at 100% so far. What you want me to do with the body?"

Patricia glanced to Davenport, "What about Blake?" She asked.

Alfa team leader glanced to Davenport for a second, "Erm… any survivors?"

Bravo team leader then watched one of his men approach the sitting secretary, and pointed a gun at her head, executing her. She collapsed with a thud.

"I'd hazard a guess at no, Alfa, but we haven't covered the whole station yet."

Patricia's heart sank. She had already feared the worst when Darren's radio failed to respond.

"Ok, we'll bag this one up, and get the lab to run some tests." Bravo team leader concluded, and clipped his radio to his belt again.

He knelt down to Sarah, who lay half curled up with her face to the floor, and reached for her shoulder. Suddenly she reacted, lashing out with one hand and the Bravo leader's head was severed. His body spasmed as the head hit the floor and rolled down the corridor. The two other SWAT cops cried out, then Sarah leaped into the air, jumping onto the chest of one, biting into his neck, and releasing a geyser of blood. The officer at the far end of the corridor watched in terror, slowly raising his pistol with shaking hands. Just then, a figure walked out of an office door ahead of him, blocking his view.

"Hey man, out of the way!!!" the officer yelled.

The man then raised a hand as if to order him to hold. It was Darren. He walked forward slowly, the shotgun in his hands, a finger on the trigger.

"Sarah." He then shouted, stopping a short distance behind.

Slowly, Sarah climbed down from the still jolting officer, who collapsed leaving his colleague to back off in total terror. She then gradually turned, hooves clicking on the hard flooring, and looked at Darren. Focusing on his face, her evil expression dropped, and for a moment, a look of innocence painted itself.

"Forgive me." Darren then said, and blasted her in the face, decapitating her in an instant, and her headless body staggered backwards, fell against the wall, before sliding to the floor.

Minutes later, Patricia exited an elevator with Davenport and two more SWAT cops. She followed Davenport up the corridor, as a panic-stricken Alfa team leader led the way.

"We lost communication. There must have been a problem." He said, as he entered the next corridor, and looked ahead to see the surviving, nervous SWAT cop resting against a wall, several feet from Sarah's naked, headless corpse.

"Jeeze." Alfa team leader gasped as he met up with the officer.

"Anderson! What happened?"

"He... killed her. Jameson is with him right now." the officer replied tearfully.

"Who? Who's Jameson with?"

"I dunno, some guy, came out of nowhere."

Patricia looked hopeful, "Blake!" She gasped and rushed forward, despite Davenport reaching out to her, but she pulled away and entered the next corridor.

She spotted Darren, slumped on the floor against the wall, sobbing his heart out. The shotgun was laid out beside him, the remaining SWAT cop standing close by.

"I can't get any sense out of him, Miss. Do you know this guy?" He asked.

Patricia hurried forward, immediately dropping to her knees and took Darren in her arms, for the second time since they had arrived in Miami. She didn't say anything, just holding him, as he gripped her tightly, crying into her shoulder. Words were pointless.

Epilogue

Eight months, two weeks later

Barrowmont Centre of Therapy,
Palmetto Bay, Florida

Patricia Willis walked down a corridor; hair cropped short with a blue slide through it, and was wearing an oversized dress with simple sandals. She was heavily pregnant, and she caught the eye of the middle-aged receptionist as she returned to the foyer. A set of double doors ahead beamed in the brightness of day, and she noticed rain falling on the street beyond. A simple denim jacket had been hung over one arm, and in reaction, she opened it out and went to put it on.

Suddenly she froze. Her eyes widened, then she grunted, and a torrent of water flooded the floor around her. Embarrassed, she looked around herself, then smirked as the receptionist stood up in alarm.

She hurried out from behind the counter, then stopped on seeing the water, "Miss? She remarked.

"A little help here please. I think I'm having my baby." Patricia said, trembling slightly as she felt a terrible pressure in her abdomen.

Somewhat nervously, the receptionist nodded then hurried away, whilst Patricia staggered back to the counter, resting against it. Her face was flushed, and she had begun to perspire.

Shortly afterwards, Patricia was in the back of an ambulance, the muffled noise of the siren blaring overhead, and the vehicle rumbled with motion. A female paramedic was positioned between Patricia's legs, which were open and bent at the knees.

"You're a little dilated, but there's plenty of time yet – don't worry about a thing, Miss Willis." She remarked, and Patricia smiled at her, then held a cell phone to her ear.

It was taken out of her hand by a male paramedic, who switched it off, "I'm sorry ma'am, you can't use that in here.

Are there any relatives or perhaps your husband we can notify, once we're at the hospital?"

Patricia sighed breathlessly.

"In situations like this, we normally call the baby's father. Do you have the number, Miss Willis?" the female Paramedic added.

Patricia closed her eyes. It was starting to hurt. She sighed again, before grabbing the male paramedic's arm.

"It's on my cell, look for the name 'Blake'…" She gasped, then opened her eyes, looking at the female paramedic with anticipation.

"It's alright Miss Willis. You're doing just fine."

"Erm, can I have my arm back, ma'am?"

Patricia looked to the male paramedic, then released his arm, smiling.

"Are you hoping for a boy or a girl?" the female paramedic asked.

Patricia looked back to her, "At this moment honey, I don't care – I just want it out."

The female paramedic looked to her colleague with concern, and Patricia closed her eyes again, exhaling through her nose, then suddenly slipped into unconsciousness. The male paramedic looked at her, and grabbed her hand, tapping it gently.

"Miss Willis… Patricia… can you hear me?"

His words faded, drifting away as all around her went black.

Patricia found herself walking through a bright, sun-drenched meadow, cherry blossom falling from trees on either side, and up ahead she noticed a figure. She felt euphoric, at peace, almost floating as she trod the blades of grass with bare feet, a gentle breeze blowing a simple flowery dress around her legs.

She reached the figure and smiled to see it was Darren. Yet he did not appear to reflect how she was feeling, the exact opposite in fact, his face forlorn and his eyes looking down.

"Blake?" She said, her voice echoey and ethereal.

Darren looked at her, and it was obvious he had been crying.

"He's dead." Darren replied.

"Who is?"

"Blake Thomas."

Patricia frowned, "I don't understand."

"Who was I kidding? I'm Darren Maitland, and always will be, no matter how much I fight against it. I can't turn my back on the past any longer, Patricia. I've been living a lie."

"Hey, don't talk like that. It's going to be ok; you've come a long way since what happened." Patricia reassured, and stepped forward, taking his hands in hers.

She grimaced to discover a wet feel to them, and let go, raising her own hands to find blood coating the palms, "What is this?" She asked.

Darren then held a hand up, as it dripped blood, "This means something, Patricia. It's a message. This isn't over." He replied.

Patricia stepped back, a horrible feeling flooding through her.

"You're wrong. It's just a dream."

"No, Patricia. It's never just a dream."

*

Several hours later, Patricia was sitting up in a hospital bed, replaying the dream over and over inside her head. She looked around the bright white room, it's very presence ethereal. A knock came to the door, and it opened to reveal a young nurse, her smile gradually relaxing Patricia.

"Miss Willis … I think there's someone who wants to meet you." She said, then walked in, opening the door wide, and Patricia sat up, tired yet feeling relieved.

Maybe the dream didn't mean a thing – it wasn't like she hadn't dreamt similar things before. She was worrying over nothing. She smiled back at the nurse, then saw another nurse walk in, holding her baby wrapped in a white blanket. Butterflies danced in her stomach. She had looked to this day with more anticipation than any other in her life. She focused on the large black nurse who then brought her baby over and grinned in reply, handing Patricia her first child. A cute, wrinkled face looked up at her, eyes barely open. As Patricia held the baby, she could feel the little legs and feet moving within the blanket. For the first time in her life, she felt complete. She couldn't be happier.

"We were quite worried for a moment back there, what with you passing out. If you hadn't have come round in time for the birth, we may have had to perform a caesarean." the young nurse announced.

Patricia couldn't shift her gaze from her child, not really listening. She touched the tiny nose and ran a finger across the cheek. Nobody else mattered anymore – nobody else existed.

"Miss…" the black nurse said, overshadowing the bed.

After a moment, Patricia looked up.

"Yes?"

"There's a man outside, asking to see you."

Patricia frowned, "Oh?"

"Should I let him come in?"

"Why not?"

The black nurse smiled, then walked out. The other nurse re-arranged some flowers in a vase.

"These are nice, who sent them?"

"My sister." Patricia replied.

The nurse then looked back to see the door creak open again, and Darren entered, lingering a few feet from the end of the bed.

"Patricia…" He said, staring at her with affection.

"Blake! What are you doing over there? Come over and meet my little girl." Patricia replied.

Darren smiled, but didn't move.

"I've got some news. I'm going away."

Patricia recognised the expression on his face; unmistakably similar to the one he had in her dream.

"What are you talking about?"

"I've left it long enough already; I have to sort some things out. I'm not sure how long that's going to take, but I will be back. I promise."

"Just come here and look at my daughter, will you?" Patricia said, and Darren approached, reaching the bedside, and looked to the little face within the blanket.

"What name you chosen for her?"

Patricia stared at the child, mesmerised and said, "Jessica. I thought I'd call her Jessica."

Darren looked at Patricia, liking the sentiment, being the same name as the little girl who had died, "Oh right. That, that's perfect, Patricia."

Patricia smiled, "I thought so."

Darren then leaned over and kissed Patricia on her head, "Be well, Patricia." He said, and then went to walk away.

Patricia looked to him, "Where you going?"

"I have a flight to catch. I'll be in touch."

"Just be careful, do you promise me?" Patricia added.

Darren returned a smile, before leaving through the door, and Patricia pondered the moment before looking at Jessica once again.

Many thanks for reading 'Forever Midnight'.

I am very proud of this story, my attempt at an erotic horror that I hope was both sexy and scary! It was also my chance to bring the character of Patricia Willis, a background character in my Dying Games Saga, to the forefront, as she has been a character I've used many times in the past, and whom you will see much more of in the future.

Please remember to rate me on Amazon, and if you wish, leave me a review.
I also hope you will seek out my other novels.

Craig.

Craig Micklewright

Prepare for... **Origin**

Printed in Great Britain
by Amazon